Chapman 8

Window on Cata

Illustrations by Alfons Bytautus, Jane Dunlop and David Schofield.

ISBN 0 906772 84 2   ISSN 0308-2695   © *Chapman* 1997

CHAPMAN
4 Broughton Place, Edinburgh EH1 3RX, Scotland
E-mail: chapman@compura.com.uk
Tel 0131–557 2207   Fax 0131–556 9565

Editor: Joy Hendry   **Assistant Editor: Gerry Stewart**

Volunteers: Valerie Brotherton, John Edwards, Isla Lillie, C J Lindsay,
Colin Mackay, Lisa Morton, Emma Pitcairn.

Submissions:

Chapman welcomes submissions of poetry, fiction and articles provided they are accompanied by a stamped addressed envelope or International Reply Coupons

Subscriptions:

	Personal		Institutional	
	1 year	2 years	1 year	2 years
UK	£15	£28	£20	£37
Overseas	£20/$34	£37/$62	£25/$42	£45/$74

THE SCOTTISH ARTS COUNCIL

•EDINBVRGH•
THE CITY OF EDINBURGH COUNCIL

Printed by Inglis Allen, Middlefield Road, Falkirk FK2 9AG

Editorial

More than ever, given the overwhelmingly positive Referendum result and the real possibility of creating a new Scotland, formed by a new cultural, social and political vision, it is vital to look elsewhere in the world, to learn from other people's strengths, their problems and their solutions to them. It is especially valuable to do this when there are discernible parallels between Scotland and other countries or communities of a broadly similar nature. Catalonia is an obvious example, one often referred to in the Referendum debate. In some ways, because of the focus on language, Catalonia may have more in common with Wales, but in the potency of its political attitudes, may more directly resemble what Scotland may become, given our proposed Parliament.

It is therefore especially welcome that the first *Chapman* to be assembled since the Referendum is devoted to Catalan literature, compiled and translated by Christopher Whyte, novelist, poet and lecturer in Scottish literature at Glasgow University. The strength of the Catalan language has been a major factor in the Catalonian battle for greater autonomy, and a huge literary strength. Catalan has survived the oppression of the Franco years, building itself up again despite onslaught from the media, languages like Spanish and English that lay claim to the international airwaves. This example gives us heart that our minority indigenous languages, Scots and Gaelic, have a future in the world of the new millennium.

It is heartening too to note the similarity of some of their problems to ours. There is a debate about the quality of Catalan spoken today, as opposed to that of 40 years ago – very like discussions about the Gaelic and Scots spoken by our younger generations, with all the linguistic implications about what is or is not 'genuine' speech. There is also the interesting parallel that Catalan women feel a double impediment, one stemming from gender and the other from being part of a minority, disadvantaged community, very like to what I have identified in previous essays as "the double knot in the peeny" syndrome. One of the most exciting opportunities offered in the new Scotland is the increased possibility of international dialogue (so much for narrow nationalism!) and I feel this Catalan feature is, for us, a small but inspiring step in that direction.

Looking back to the previous *Chapman* issue, Jon Corelis's article about the State of British Poetry, quite deliberately an outsider's view, with all its potential for misrepresentation, impressionism, even downright uniformed prejudice, has provoked strong responses. Building on this, we intend in a future issue to fuel this debate by inviting people to submit their responses to the piece. This analyses British poetry into five distinct schools, the Scottish school (which he suggested was his preferred area – without any editorial bribery or priming!), the Suburbanites, the Urbanites, the Academics and the Starters Over. We invite readers to address the question of just how healthy British poetry really is, what are its strengths and its inadequacies. Responses should not exceed 1,000 words without prior consultation with the *Chapman* team. We look forward to a stimulating and vigorous debate.

Window on Catalonia

Christopher Whyte

It was the generosity of the Royal Society of Edinburgh which allowed me to spend three months in Barcelona on a Humanities Research Fellowship early in 1996. Thanks to good Italian and reasonable French, reading Catalan was never a problem. Learning to speak the language took rather longer, with those first person singular verbs ending in a consonant (so odd for a Romance language) and the need to clip unstressed vowels, so as to approximate the characteristically throaty Catalan timbre.

An observation of Milan Kundera's, encountered many years ago in his essay 'Prague: a disappearing poem', was part inspiration for my visit: "The Europe made up of little countries is *another* Europe", he writes. "It offers another perspective and its culture is often completely at odds with the Europe of big countries." If Scotland and Catalonia were both little countries, would their perspective on things be the same? Would their cultures be structured in similar ways, echoing one another? A less reverent inspiration was Terenci Moix's *The Sex of Angels*, a hugely funny, satirical and nonetheless affectionate portrayal of arty Barcelona at the end of the 1960s.

But if I felt so at home in the city, could that be because its biculturalism, an unaffected bilingualism (among Catalan speakers!) I have encountered nowhere else in Europe, was a comfortable and relaxed reflection of the Glasgow I grew up in, divided between two communities, two religions, two nationalities almost? The conclusion of my researches was heartening, if surprising. Even if the restrictions they have laboured under are not dissimilar, Scotland and Catalonia are very different societies. Oppressive forces are not so powerful as to dictate the nature of our response to them, numbing the creativity of those they are directed against. If the Europe of little countries is another Europe, it is not uniform and any dialogue between its members, while it may touch on shared issues, will be a dialogue from very distinct positions.

The essays here were commissioned specially for *Chapman*. Josep Maria Murgades, who has done major work on Pompeu Fabra's standardisation of the Catalan language, teaches at the Central University in Barcelona, and puts forward a radical perspective. Neus Real, currently completing a research project at the Autonomous University, argues that certain feminist positions reinforce the marginalisation they claim to be attacking and makes a plea to 'normalise' the apparently dual 'abnormality' of being a woman who writes in Catalan. Lluís-Maria Todó, author of three novels and a lecturer at the Pompeu Fabra University, takes a theatre production as the basis for reflections on the future of his language which, if they may strike Scottish readers as unduly gloomy, are not untypical of Catalan intellectuals today.

Quim Monzó and Sergi Pàmies are among the foremost and most successful practitioners of fiction, especially short fiction, in the Catalan language. Their wryly humorous view of sexual and social cavortings in middle-class Barcelona has made them both immensely popular. The tone of their work could hardly be further from political correctness or nar-

4

rowly doctrinaire nationalist commitment. Interrogated for the umpteenth time about the health of Catalan writing, Monzó has compared it irreverently to Nepalese (on which he is not considered to be an expert. Was he protesting about a 'Nepalisation' of Catalan literature by outsiders?) We are grateful to their publisher, Quaderns Crema, for permission to include a sample of short stories here.

Gabriel Ferrater, who killed himself in 1972 at the age of 50, is an emblematic figure for Catalan writing in the years preceding the end of the dictatorship. His long poem 'In Memoriam' offers an acerbic, unheroic account of one adolescent's experience of the Civil War, a salutary antidote to victimology which refuses to simplify the extremely complex affiliations and alignments of that tragic period. Renowed as an artist and a writer for the theatre, Narcís Comadira, born in Girona in 1942, speaks with a contrasting voice in his poetry: ironic yet tender, disenchanted yet romantic, engaged in an intimate yet fascinating game of self-reflection and self-criticism. Maria-Mercè Marçal won widespread acclaim for her first novel, *The Passion According to Renée Vivien*, published in 1995. Until then she had confined herself to poetry, as well as being a founding member of the important series of publications 'Llibres del Mall'. Her verse has a riveting intensity which does not avoid closed forms but draws strength from them. The translator's sense of personal inadequacy prevented him attempting the sestinas of 'Terra de Mai' which chronicle a tempestuous love affair. The poems included come from *Sister, Stranger*, a volume which describes the experience of childbirth along with the erotic tensions provoked by the figure of a midwife.

A word of warning. This selection observes a distinction fundamental in Barcelona which may yet surprise a Scottish public. Catalan literature is literature written in the Catalan language. A writer born and bred in the city, who spends his or her whole life there but writes in Spanish, is not considered a Catalan, but a Spanish writer. And because the aim of the selection is to give a flavour of what is happening in Barcelona today, this distinction is not discussed or questioned but, quite simply, reproduced.

All texts are my own translations from the Catalan. I apologise in advance for any oversights or inaccuracies which may have escaped my attention. The project could not have been completed without the generous assistance of a whole range of friends in Barcelona. In particular I want to thank Jaume Subirana for his untiring enthusiasm and advice, and Paddy McAree for his courteous, permissive and uninvasive hospitality.[1]

4

---

1. The originals of the published texts translated here can be found in: Sergi Pàmies 'Caixa oberta' and 'Sucursal' in *T'hauria de caure la cara de vergonya* (Barcelona, Quaderns Crema 1986) pp 91-100 & 7-14; Quim Monzó 'Vida matrimonial' and 'Quarts d'una' in *El perquè de tot plegat* (Barcelona, Quaderns Crema 1992) pp 21-24 & 99-116; Gabriel Ferrater *Les dones i els dies* (Barcelona, Edicions 62 1989) pp 15-23; Maria-Mercè Marçal *Llengua abolida 1973-1988* (Valencia, Poesia 3i4 1989) pp 331, 337, 338, 341-343, 347, 356; Narcís Comadira *Somnis i runa* (Barcelona, Edicions Proa 1992) pp 11, 16-17, 60-61, 135-136, and *Usdefruit* (Barcelona, Editorial Empúries 1995) pp 35, 54.

Cashline
Sergi Pàmies

I insert the card as indicated and wait. The screen lights up and welcomes me to the 24 hour cashline service. It is two o'clock in the morning. The welcome fades and a thoroughly polite message appears asking me to key in my personal identification number. I press the appropriate keys and the machine's response is immediate and precise: I have to choose the operation I want. There are six possible ones, and obviously I choose "cash withdrawal". It beats me how anyone could want anything else. The screen wants to know the exact amount. I manage to get it right. Now the thing is to see if everything is correct. I proceed. For a moment there is no message and then, at last, a series of characters informs me that the operation is in process. I am pleased. I can hear the bowels of the machine digesting my orders, shredding information, storing and summarising the details in minuscule characters which explain the branch, the day and the time. The text changes. Apparently the cashline cannot take any responsibility for the use I may make of the required sum. I do not understand. I read the phrase again and conclude this is an effect of the latest measures to raise moral standards in the country. But the money fails to emerge. The message is repeated intermittently, combined with others telling me the central office wants to know *why* I need to withdraw money at two o'clock in the morning. As there is no key which permits the customer to send them to hell, I try to stay calm and wait for the next set of instructions. Tomorrow I will pay the bank clerk a visit and remind him about "withdrawing money, immediately, at any of our branches". The machine shakes like a washing-machine and orders me to take back my card. No print out, no money Nothing.

A green telephone for complaints is situated to the right of the screen. I pick it up. A robotic voice asks me where I am calling from and what the problem is. I answer that the automatic cashline at branch number 30 and I are not seeing eye to eye. The voice asks me to explain. I give an exaggerated summary of how indignant I am while also supplying the most humiliating details of the episode. The voice tells me they will send someone right away. I hang up. A man not wearing mechanic's trousers and without a hostile expression on his face smiles at me from behind the glass panes. He is the technician. He is dressed in sea blue and seems ready to be amiable and efficient. He shows me a document proving he is a specialist in night breakdowns. His name is Virgili.

"The photograph was taken several years ago," he comments. "I still had a moustache then."

He opens his case and asks me to hold his jacket. He wants me to show him my card. I tell him that if the identification number is personal and secret he will not be able to set the machine going. Unaffected, he inserts the card in the appropriate place and waits. The screen lights up and welcomes him to the 24 hour cashline service. It is half past two in the morning. I tell him that now the text will fade and he will have to key in my number.

"I know," he says, and presses the right keys.

"But isn't it secret?" I ask indignantly.

"No," he answers, as if he were speaking to a fool.

Without consulting me, he decides he wants to withdraw two thousand pesetas. Like an old hand he repeats all the operations until the screen says it cannot take any responsibility for the use that may be made of the required sum. Virgili stops. He leafs through his book of instructions nervously and confesses, without looking up, that the latest rule forbids withdrawing money after a certain time, and that they will more than likely make me explain *why* I want to take money out at half past two in the morning.

"And how am I supposed to talk to this machine?" I ask.

"By phone," he answers, giving me my card back.

"Can I lie?"

"No," he says, and closes his bag with a resigned gesture.

"And what happens if I say I need money to get pissed?"

"I wouldn't advise you to do that."

He is very upset. Without daring to look at me he says he is awfully sorry. I should look on the situation as temporary, probably the result of some mix-up.

"I'll have a go in any case," I say, to cheer him up a bit.

"Do whatever you like," he says, but waits.

I pick up the phone. The robotic voice asks exactly the same question and I answer that, to begin with, what I do with *my* money is none of their bloody business, but if they really want to know, I will tell them that my daughter is dying of a haemorrhage in a taxi and I need money to get her into hospital urgently. Certainly no less than two thousand pesetas.

"A pack of lies," says the voice.

"It's to buy drink then!" I shout. Virgili can do nothing to stop me.

The voice informs me that that is what was feared. Buying drink is an unacceptable vulgarity. The thing people do now is play at roulette or withdraw money to give to the hungry.

No way. Virgili bites his nails. He is getting extremely down about it all. I try to console him: the way things are, I would be quite happy to abandon the drink and go straight home. He says it is not right. For two months now he has had to defend the rule to customers and if people cannot do what they want with their own money, where will it all end?

"They want to put an end to night life," I say, just to say something.

But he is not listening to me. He takes his jacket and gets two thousand pesetas from his wallet.

"Here," he offers.

"Not on any account. I'm serious. I cannot accept it … "

But he will not listen. He says I can give the money back and please not to make a fuss over it. From his tone of voice it is more of an order than a proposal. The situation is complicated. If I take the money, each time I have a drink I will think about poor Virgili and there will be no way I can get my spirits up. On the other hand, if I go home because of the bloody rule, I will get very depressed, maybe even more so. Solution: to get pissed together. I put it to him and he agrees at once.

We drive across the city in his van to a trendy bar: a former tannery converted into a bar with three mobile counters and two dance floors. Virgili has never been there. Me neither. We park in a pedestrian area and follow the flood of people struggling to get in. A pair of willowy photo models are on the door. There are problems with an old man who is not sufficiently well dressed and gets thrown out violently. We manage to get right up in front of the two human palm trees with their earrings and drawling accents.

"We want in," says Virgili.

"Everybody wants in," one of them answers. "Do you have a membership card?"

"No, but we can pay."

"To pay you either have to be a member or be invited."

"So what is the advantage of being a member?" I ask.

"They get to pay," the other answers.

"I left my invitation at home, but I'm a close friend of Kuki and Lys," I lie.

"Lys?" one of them asks the other.

"Yes," I say. "The really tall redhead who lives with the disc jockey."

The men on the door look at each other and ask us to wait next to the pillar. One of them goes in to check out the disc jockey's private life.

From where we are, we can observe the members filing past, showing off the latest novelties in dress and perfume. Rubber overcoats, metallic blouses, fibreglass trousers, porcelain belts and a terrifying range of badges. The doorman comes out again and tells us the disc jockey is a homosexual who has lived all his life with his parents.

"There must be some mistake," I say.

The bouncers, however, will not be taken in. Virgili, silent up to now, demands to speak with the manager. The doorman tells him the manager is too busy to waste time with all the no gooders who try to force their way in and will we please stop blocking the entrance. A girl emerges from the bar asking where *her* taxi is. She is wearing a peculiar hat: it is an open telephone directory, with a stainless steel crest. Virgili looks at me in astonishment and asks:

"He called us no gooders, didn't he?"

"I'm afraid he did."

He takes his hands out of his pockets, closes his fist resolutely and hits the doorman in the face. As if he had been doing this all his life, the other whistles, and three Dobermanns appear from a side exit. In spite of years of training and a sense of smell trained for every kind of killing, they cannot tell who their victims are. There is a moment of panic and we take the chance to get out of the mess. The girl with the hat turns round on seeing the dogs and starts to scream hysterically. With frothing mouths they jump at her throat. Before falling, the girl shouts:

"But I'm carrying a membership card!"

By the time the Dobermanns realise they are mauling a member, we are already in the van and the girl is well and truly dead. At the wheel, Virgili curses bouncers and cashline machines.

"They belong to the same breed," he says, pressing the accelerator.

Jumping the lights at high speed we go back to the old part of town. We park in front of a bar lit by a green sign saying: "Babylon". We go in. This is not an old tannery. A narrow bar curves down to a tiny dance floor where a negro[1] is gesticulating and drinking beer. There is also a fat man painting his nails. A toothless waiter welcomes us with a smile.

"Hello, good lookers ... "

We ask for two martinis. Virgili pays. He takes his jacket off and asks me to forgive him for the way he treated the doorman in the other bar. He is smiling.

"I'm not always that violent," he says, and puts a hand on my leg.

I do not move. I do not like "Babylon". We talk about his work and I notice the man moving perilously closer. The negro asks for another beer. The toothless waiter tells him he has drunk enough already. The negro insists. The fat man says: "Here we are again" and goes off to the dance floor. Virgili grabs the negro by the neck and advises him to get lost. I tell him to pay no attention to what the negro does. Virgili tells me not to go seeking *more* problems and that if the waiter does not want to give him more beer the other man should not insist. I say nothing. Knowing how he reacts, I prefer not to have him smash my face in. The negro reaches the same conclusion: he pays and leaves. The fat man comes back to the bar. Virgili expresses the opinion that negroes belong dragging their cocks in the sand. He and the waiter laugh. I do not say a thing. Before he can take my hand I say:

"I need a pee."

The window of the toilets gives onto an inner courtyard. I jump. I walk beside the wall, as far as the wire fence which opens onto the lane. With a kick, I break the chain and, running, put a distance between me, the toothless waiter, Virgili and the poof at the bar.

I do not have enough money to take a taxi. On the Ramblas, I ask for small change to catch a bus but nobody wants to give me any. I turn my pockets out but all I can find is my identity card and the cashline card. It is four o'clock in the morning.

---

1. The Catalan term "moro" is not politically correct.

Illustration by Alfons Bytautas

Married Life

Quim Monzó

Because they have some papers to sign, Zgdt and his wife Bst (who got married eight years ago) have to travel to a distant city. They get there in the early evening. As the business cannot be settled till the next day, they look for a hotel where they can spend the night. They are given a room with twin beds, two bedside cabinets, a writing table (there are envelopes and sheets of paper with the hotel's name at the top, in a folder), a chair and a minibar with a television on top of it. They have dinner, take a walk along the river bank and, when they get back to the hotel, each gets into one of the beds and takes out a book.

A few minutes later they can hear people fucking in the room next door. They hear distinctly the mattress creaking, the woman's groans and, more faintly, the panting of the man. Zgdt and Bst look at one another, smile, make a joke about it, bid each other good night and put the light out. Zgdt is turned on, as he can still hear them fucking on the other side of the wall, and he wonders about saying something to Bst. Maybe she is turned on just like him. He could go over, sit down on her bed, make a joke about the people next door and, without any fuss, start by stroking her hair and her face and then, immediately afterwards, her breasts. Very probably, Bst would respond right away. But if she doesn't? If she pushes his hand away and clucks with her tongue or, worse still, says: "I'm not in the mood?" A few years ago he would not have hesitated. He would have known, just before putting out the light, whether Bst wanted to, whether the groans from the room next door had turned her on or not. But now that so many years have gone by, nothing is clear. Zgdt turns to one side and masturbates, being careful not to make any noise.

Ten minutes after he has finished, Bst asks him if he is asleep. Zgdt says not yet. They have stopped groaning in the room next door; now they are talking in low voices, with suppressed laughter. Bst gets up and comes over to Zgdt's bed. She lifts the sheet, lies down and starts caressing his back. Her hand descends from his back to his buttocks. Zgdt does not have the courage to tell her he has just masturbated and says he is not in the mood. Bst stops caressing him and, after a short, very long silence, gets back into her bed. He hears her lifting the sheet, getting in, turning over. Feeling more courageous, Zgdt turns towards her and confesses that, a few minutes ago, he masturbated because he thought she wouldn't feel like fucking. Bst says nothing.

Not long afterwards, Zgdt deduces, from the disguised noises reaching him, that Bst is masturbating. Zgdt feels a huge sadness, reflects that life is grotesque and unjust, and bursts into tears. He cries into the pillow, thrusting his head as deeply into it as he can. The tears are plentiful and hot. And when he hears Bst stifling the final groan with the palm of her hand, he moans with the very moan she bites back.

Gabriel Ferrater

In Memoriam

When the war broke out, I was fourteen
years and two months old. To begin with
it had practically no effect
on me. My head was stuffed with something else,
which even now I see as being more
significant, discovering *Les Fleurs
du Mal,* and that meant poetry, of course.
There is another element, however,
the one that really matters, which I can't
find words for. Revolt? No, even if that's what
I called it then. Stretched out flat inside
a hazel grove, at the heart of a rose
whose leaves resembled, limp and very green,
caterpillar skins that had been peeled
off, bedded there in the crutch of the world,
happy revolt grew thicker and thicker
inside me, while the country echoed with
the shots of revolt and counter-revolt,
I cannot tell whether happy or not,
but more rebellious than I was. Life on
the moral plane? That comes quite close, but has
an air of ambiguity for me.
The best word for it might be egoism,
and it is worth remembering that when
we reach the age of fourteen we are forced
to change first person habits, since the plural
already fits us rather tightly, and
the singular stylite, a nauseous
ascent to the top of oneself, appears
a good plan for the future. Then the years
come and, happily, also depart,
our hand increasingly grows tired as it
fondles the stubborn forehead of the lamb
within, and we find ourselves adopting
this plural, which I cannot securely
define as modest, and which renounces
the singular, abandoning it, while
thanking and rewarding it. Enough.
          Once the holidays were finished, yes,
I saw someone had battered my world's face
into a new shape. Blood and fire. They did
not strike me as horrific, but they were

the blood and fire of every age. They burned
the priests' school that I studied in, and Guiu,
the sergeant we all hated, who took us
for gym in preparation for the army,
(I go back to the first person plural
because life always travels backwards) had
been shot and killed. They told us that it was
a major undertaking, as he wore
a coat of chain mail when he went disguised
as an old peasant woman, and hid three
grenades beneath the eggs he carried in
his basket. They shot him on the corner
of the Placeta d'Hèrcules, beside
the institute, where we used to come out
to spend the break between two lessons. I
cannot remember that we found the place
altered in the slightest, or that we
looked for a bullet in a plane-tree trunk
or any other evidence. As for
the blood, what need is there to say the wind
carried it off, maybe that very day?
Maybe the dust was a bit heavier
as a result, that's all. I cannot tell
for certain if I do remember how
the college walls were blackened, or if I
merely think I do. We never entered.
We were sloughing off our skins, and had
no interest in the tatters of the old one.
Our nostrils were filled with the fear which was
the perfume of that autumn, and yet it
struck us as good. It was an adult fear.
We were emerging from our childish fear
and, luckily for us, our world became
almost totally easy. The more fear
they experienced, the freer we
felt. It was the same old story, and
we vaguely sensed that, in our case, the wheel
was turning ever faster. We were happy.
    Happy all together, always, very.
They made us join a trade union, and it
gave us various and stimulating
pleasures. In a requisitioned flat,
for us an enemy flat that we had
occupied (I mean our enemy,
not the official one) behind the smoke
from poker tables, we removed both books
and furniture, and bartered guns and bullets,

exchanged Roman salutes (there was no special
reason for this, we preferred our own side,
but the opposing one was more renowned
for wickedness), tried to lure the girls
into the corners and, because it didn't
work, disgruntled, used the balcony
for our entries and exits. We discovered
whores and robbery. We would have seen
things being robbed in any case: as for
the brothels, we'd have gained admittance there
soon enough. The war saved us a few
months, however. We sat out the first
air raid sheltering in one of them
they called "la Sol", all of us terrified
of being found. Significantly shrunk,
our fathers still held power. Isidre was
the first of us to catch the clap. His father
could hardly have chosen a worse moment
to buy the bicycle he had been asking
for insistently. We had to take
turn about borrowing it from him,
providing him with an excuse for not
using it himself. My memories
of that period are filled with bicycles,
the thing we robbed most often. We set up
a full scale workshop to paint them afresh
and reassemble them, the frame from one,
another's wheels, tyres from another still.
    I don't know why, one afternoon when all
of us had slipped away from home, leaving
the day's main meal half finished, for a trip
to the castle at Tamarit, I shut
the door and was without a bicycle.
What I wanted to do was rent one, but
I found the shop they knew me at was closed.
It made me furious. I refused to give
up. I kicked the door and beat upon it
with my fists. It opened to me. There
was no-one there. I seized the bike and left
a note for them. The trip was nerve-racking.
An unremitting wind bent us double.
On the way back we had it in our faces.
Standing upright in the pedals, as
if I were climbing a steep slope, transfixed
and trembling, I struggled on, without
making progress. Gradually we lost
sight of one another. Agustí

14

and I spent ages resting in the shelter
of the ditch beside the fields that they
were levelling to make an airport out of.
We finished the return journey by night
and walking half the time. At the first houses
we found an open bakery and threw
ourselves upon it. We were kids, much more
truly kids than our age might suggest:
falling onto the chill tiles of the floor
we ate several loaves that had just come
out of the oven, burying our faces
completely in them, crazy with the pleasure
of being merely fatigue, hunger and weight.
Anything could happen, and the sudden
racket – footsteps, shouts – did not surprise me,
nor did the oily gun barrels that pointed
directly at me where I lay, nor someone
pulling me up, shoving me in a van,
nor that my father was waiting for me
in a place I did not know, engaged
in argument with lots of people, where
the fathers of my friends were waiting, too.
Little by little mine appeared to gain
the upper hand, and took me home. The next
day I understood the business
had been collectivised. The members of
the junta were incensed, and spent the whole
evening chasing after us to get
a bicycle back which its former owner
would doubtless have been more than happy to
rent out on those conditions. They were not.
Briefly, our fathers struck us as important.
        That wasn't all we robbed. For a long time
we were obsessed with underpants. A crowd
of us would walk into a shop, inspect the wares,
sort through them and buy nothing, while we crammed
our jerseys and shirts full of underpants.
I don't know what we did with them. Nor can
I understand what stopped them catching us.
The likeliest explanation is that at
the time they constantly suffered a sort
of seasickness, were shocked and perhaps
twisted, too, so that their sense of order
had been affected. They were indifferent
to being robbed, or else it turned them on.
All we knew was that the shopkeepers
gave into us with eyes that watered, like

a woman who is vanquished by her rapist.
I remember one day our choice fell
on Subietes' shop again, a place
we often visited and never left
empty-handed. The owner himself served
us, laid the boxes out upon the counter,
opened them, and when he took them back
out of our reach, counted up all the items
aloud. We returned them without insisting
and he counted them over again. When we
emerged, swollen with pride, I showed the pair
of underpants I'd taken at the start,
before he counted them the first time. And
that was not all: Albert had taken more.
They all slept, with a crackling in their ears.
     Subietes, too, died violently. If now
I think of him, I see black and white clothes,
worn by someone who looked really old.
Maybe he wasn't. As goes for the black,
I don't think it was mourning: the man couldn't
keep away from mass, and in those days
all churchgoers wore black, as did a few
older men who cared about their clothes,
along with a Republican or two,
the kind who never wavered all their lives.
Old Subietes went to jail because
he was a Catholic. His luck had run out.
After they had taken him off, one day
huge panic broke out. The Italians were
at Salou. They'd already disembarked.
Our local junta requisitioned three
or four coaches, put in the prisoners
they held and drove them to a ditch
at the roadside. It happened very quickly
and took up no more time than that imagined
peril. One of the drivers requisitioned
with their coaches, who had to spectate,
was Ton. Out of the corner of his eyes,
he watched, appalled, as one after another
the passengers alighting brushed against
his seat in passing by. He knew them all,
or nearly all. Mr Subietes saw
the horror in Ton's face, and was affected
by it. On the point of getting out,
he halted for a moment, placed his hand
upon Ton's shoulder, and told him: "You see
the pass that things have reached, Tonet." Scant comfort.

I also knew the man responsible
for that day's massacre, the junta's leader.
    Oliva is the man I want to talk
about now. He had been, before the war,
doorkeeper at the cinema we went
to every Sunday, the Sala Reus, where
we'd taint our hands with love. I haven't seen
him since then. The one image that I have
of him is wearing leather, carrying
a Luger with a butt of pale wood, longer
than his thigh, making it seem more like
a banner than a weapon. War provokes
a hankering for symbols. Both of them
loved rituals, Oliva and his wife.
They commandeered a wealthy family's mansion
and settled there. Immediately she
decided that important people had
to decorate their house with cactus plants.
She'd come to see in them a sign of what's
superfluous in rich people's lives, the merest
shadow of a soul, beneath the huge
sun of ownership. She was the one
who owned things now, and laughed, the women all
laughed, and bought life turned a commodity,
material at last, trimmed of its hopes.
The moment only lasted two or three
months, in which the women of the people
went around laughing, feeling no surprise
at how things were. They'd always laughed that way.
Hope came back to them, and buying was
a thing you did in secret, practised by
the rich more than the poor. We reached the turning
point, and the road back was gradually
hemmed in by boundaries we recognised.
I often saw Oliva and the other
members of the junta sitting at
a café table, waiting for each other,
or rushing down a street to sit and wait
    One evening we had a symphony concert.
My father took me to it, and I was
so impatient I shook from head to toe.
Music *parfois nous prend comme une mer.*
The sea that overwhelmed me that night was
of an epoch about to be lost, one
you could see disappearing, taking back
the things that it had promised. The idea
of yielding myself to another current,

more personal, at any rate without
companions other than my father, filled
me with excitement. Beethoven, Ravel
were the composers that I heard, and if
they overwhelmed me, I cannot tell now
what destination they impelled me towards.
Once the concert was over, they played anthems:
Riego, the Internationale, the Reapers,
the Anarchist song that the FAI had taken
as their own tune. Oliva disapproved,
and poked his head out from the stage's edge,
shouting. So as not to hear, we clapped
more loudly still. Oliva watched the faces
laughing at him, and he went on shouting,
noiselessly, like a flame. All of us laughed,
applauded, spilled over into a stream.
The way friends do (and afterwards my father
and I really were friends) we put off going
home, and sat together over coffee.
We spoke of politics: it seems to me
that then it seemed to me there was no need
for a revolt of any kind (it is
not politics I have in mind), that young
and old could form one single, happy group.
At night time, in a café, it's OK
to have a father. Oliva came in.
Now I would realise he'd taken three
or four glasses too many. We were sitting
next to the door, and he saw us at once.
Clutching his gun's huge butt, so that it helped him
keep his balance, looking at my father,
"You," he said, "you were the one who did it."
(In those days it was a ubiquitous
pursuit to hunt for guilty parties, though
the charge was never clear. No matter what
it was confronted them, they looked around
for someone who was guiltier than the others.)
My father managed, with a scattered phrase
or two, to shift the man's attention, and
Oliva let the butt go. Later on,
when my father explained it, their exchange
became much longer. I could not make out
his reasons for dispersing its concise
virtue. Now I fully understand
his purpose: he was trying to disperse
a mist his voice had not betrayed at all,
but which had glimmered in his eyes. A mist

that fascinated me, although I did
not give it its true name on the occasions
when it flickered in mine. I came close to it
three days later, in the corridor
at "Ca la Sol", when unexpectedly
I met Oliva face to face. When we
young men toured round the brothels, it did not
occur to us this was our rightful kingdom,
and they, carrying their pistols, furtive guests.
        Then a time arrived of multiple
journeys. Somebody was shuffling us
as if we were a pack of cards, composed
of places and of people. Six or seven
years later, without warning, Oliva
entered our lives again. My mother met him.
One evening in Bordeaux, she was at home
alone, opened the door, and found him there.
He climbed our stair because he had heard people
from his own village lived on it. He wanted
help of some kind, was working in a German
factory, he told her, at Royan,
or so I think. The building and the camp
annexed to it had been destroyed by bombs.
Oliva happened to be absent, but
he lost all he possessed, belongings, money,
everything except a life that made
no sense to him, one that he was no longer
answerable for: the Germans would
take charge of his new fate. Maybe my mother
was the last woman he spoke to who knew
a thing about him. She gave him a few items
of clothing, which perhaps he never got
to wear. Another British air raid caught him
two days later.
        Seeing I did not
immigrate to Saint Germain from Oran,
fear hardly strikes me as a major theme
for literature or for philosophy.
Many men have felt fear, that is sure,
and it is right they should be spoken of.
It should be said that Oliva felt fear,
and inspired fear in many people, not
a lot in me or in my father, more
in Ton, in other people fear as great
as that he felt himself, or even greater.

Catalan: the Historical and Social Background of a Romance Language
Josep Murgades

Descended from Latin, Catalan at present counts some ten million speakers, making it comparable numerically to both Dutch and the Scandinavian languages. In Spain, it is used in the Principality of Catalonia (capital Barcelona), the Valencia region or *País Valencià* (named after its capital) and the Balearic Islands (capital Palma de Mallorca); in France, in the Roussillon region (capital Perpignan); and throughout the Principality of Andorra, an independent state where it is the only official language.

During the Middle Ages, the backbone of the Kingdom of Aragon, a major Mediterranean power, was formed by territories which were Catalan in both language and culture. As a natural consequence of this economic ascendancy, the language reached a high degree of formal development, both in literary expression and as the unified idiom of the royal chancellery. Thanks to the work of Ramon Llull in the thirteenth century, it was the first European vernacular, other than Latin, to be used for philosophical and scientific treatises. The outstandingly beautiful literature of the same period reached its peak, towards the close of the fifteenth century, in the poetry of Ausiàs March and in *Tirant lo Blanc*, rightly considered the first modern novel. Spoken dialects differed from one another, as is the case with other European languages today, yet the unifying example of the Court made written Catalan, during the Middle Ages, one of the most consistent and (if the use of an anachronistic concept can be pardoned) 'standardised' languages of Western Europe.

With the dawn of the modern age at the beginning of the sixteenth century, the Kingdom of Aragon underwent a profound crisis which had varied causes: demographic (the arrival of the plague in the second half of the fourteenth century), political (the civil war which ravaged the Principality of Catalonia in the middle of the fifteenth century) and economic (the discovery of America by the monarchs of Castile led to the Atlantic replacing the Mediterranean as the main avenue for trade). The prolonged period of decadence which resulted dragged on till the start of the industrial revolution in the 19th century, when very different circumstances obtained.

In the meantime, two wars had been waged, and lost, against the expansionist policies of the Castilian throne. In that of the *segadors* or "reapers", half way through the seventeenth century, Catalonia, unlike Portugal during those same years, was defeated and deprived of its northern counties (Roussillon passed to France). In the War of Spanish Succession, in the first two decades of the eighteenth century, the supporters of the Austrian claim to the Spanish crown were defeated by those who backed the Bourbons. At this point, the separate institutions retained hitherto by the former Kingdom of Aragon were absorbed into Castile, whose absolutist monarchy immediately set about persecuting the Catalan language in political terms.

The industrialisation of Catalonia in the course of the 19th century set a gulf between this region and the Spanish hinterland. A striking contradiction emerged by the end of the century, since the class with the greatest economic power inside the Spanish state, the Catalan bourgeoisie, was denied even minimal influence in politics. This remained in the hands of a decadent and feudal Castilian oligarchy, incapable of shoring up a collapsing overseas empire. Catalonia had always felt itself to be different from the rest of Spain. Combined with tensions of an economic nature, this led the Catalan middle classes to set their face against the power of an obsolete and anachronistic state.

The movement known as the *Renaixença* or "Rebirth", during the middle years of the nineteenth century, was one manifestation of the growing interest in 'popular' cultures, and the idealisation of the languages associated with them, provoked by Romanticism throughout Europe. But by the end of the century, this phenomenon was becoming increasingly politicised. What set Catalonia apart was that the leaders in the battle for linguistic, cultural and, in the last analysis, national self-affirmation were not scholars, even less those at the bottom of the social pyramid, but the middle and lower middle classes, dissatisfied with the state they found themselves a part of and determined to modernise it politically and socially, as well as forcing it to recognise the diversity of languages and cultures in the territories it embraced.

It was against the background briefly outlined above that the reform of the Catalan language took place, and culminated in Pompeu Fabra's proposals for 'standardisation'. The court had gone over to Castilian in the sixteenth century. In the eighteenth century Catalan was banned from education and state administration. Yet in the nineteenth century it was still the only language spoken by the vast majority of the population. Because Castilian had absorbed all official functions, and had been adopted by the upper echelons of society, Catalan had fragmented into dialects and lacked the expressive means needed if it was to be used by an industrialised society.

Pompeu Fabra (1868-1948) was a chemical engineer as well as a linguist, formed within the school of the new grammarians. Thoroughly familiar with the work of Saussure, he assumed the task of proposing a codified form of Catalan, which would reject both archaic and populist solutions. While the former meant restoring the medieval language and ignoring the historical and the resulting linguistic changes that had occurred in the meantime, the latter proposed adopting the impoverished spoken language of the period, strongly influenced by Castilian, as a standard. Consistent with his approach, Fabra put together a model of referential language with the following main characteristics.

First, he adopted a double system (*diasistematicitat*), obviously based on the central dialect of Barcelona (given the preponderance of the capital in both population and prestige), but such that all other varieties of Catalan could recognise themselves in it, especially where crucial areas such as spelling and vocabulary were concerned.

Second, he made it as distinctive as possible (*especificitat*), in other words, he chose for the norm those elements of pronunciation, morphology, vocabulary and syntax, which differed strongly from the traditionally dominant language, Castilian, and which gave the best chance of emphasising the individual nature of Catalan.

Third, he provided an intellectual register, either by borrowing from the languages of Europe's major cultures, or by exploiting the native resources of his own language, so that Catalan would formally be suitable for use in all areas of social activity, including the highest levels of culture and scientific investigation.

At the same time, Fabra was careful to keep this work of codification within strict limits. From this point of view at least, he wanted there to be no obstacles to its spread. He also ensured that only those solutions which could be adopted in practice found a place within the norm.

Two movements provided the historical context Fabra's reform needed for its adoption. *Modernisme* struggled to transform Catalonia from a regional society rooted in tradition into a modern nation, while *Noucentisme* (literally "(championing) the 1900s") gave institutional expression to the political commitment of the Catalan middle classes. The publication of the spelling rules or *Normes Ortogràfiques* in 1913, of the *Catalan Grammar* in 1918 and of the *General Dictionary of the Catalan Language* in 1932 were milestones in this process.

The diffusion of the norm met with the support of the vast majority of intellectuals sympathetic to *Noucentisme*. However, there were no parallel innovations aimed at encouraging society at large to adopt it in place of Spanish, which continued to be the official language of the state. The establishment of a dictatorship by General Primo de Rivera, which lasted from 1923 to 1930, was a major setback in this sense, much as it satisfied the Catalan middle classes. Shaken by the social upheavals resulting from the crisis which followed the First World War, they abandoned their commitment to reform and to the Catalan nation, in favour of an apparatus of repression offered by the central power. There was a renewed campaign against the use of Catalan in crucial areas such as education, public administration and the courts, a foreshadowing of the openly genocidal policy adopted by Franco's government after the Civil War.

In 1931 the Second Republic was proclaimed in Spain. Catalan nationalists, by now largely drawn from the lower middle classes and from among skilled workers, obtained a Statute of Autonomy for Catalonia. For the first time in the modern period, Catalan gained official recognition alongside Spanish, and had access to the world of education and of public administration. The achievements of the *Generalitat* (the name of the autonomous Catalan government) under the republic were, however, totally dismantled after the victory of the rebel armed forces during the war of 1936 to 1939, which set Franco's right-wingers against the left-wingers who supported the republic.

The defeat of the latter led, in Catalonia as throughout Spain, to the establishment of a nationalist and fascist dictatorship totally opposed to civil liberties with, in Catalonia, the added aim of destroying all traces of a separate identity. There was no let up in the persecution by Franco's dictatorship, from its beginning to its end, of everything that marked Catalonia out as a nation: language, culture, literature and symbols. It was only when the Axis powers lost the Second World War and, during the postwar period, Spain was gradually drawn into international organisations, that little by little the regime permitted certain cultural activities to start up again in Catalonia, naturally within the limits of the censorship to which the whole country was subjected.

Rather than in the openly repressive policies adopted towards Catalonia by Franco's regime, the real threat to the survival of Catalonia as a nation came from some of the most crucial social changes to have affected Western society, which took place while the dictator was in power (from 1939 to 1975). There was a massive immigration of Spanish speakers, victims of long-standing economic backwardness attracted by the possibilities of employment Catalonia offered. While Catalonia had always been able to absorb immigrants, however harsh the conditions which obtained, the arrival of television in the late 1950s, naturally restricted to the Spanish language, was a major blow. It now became more or less impossible to assimilate the new arrivals linguistically and Catalan society, hitherto homogeneous in ethnic terms, split into two groups: the Catalans, speaking mainly Catalan but increasingly bilingual, and the Spanish immigrants, totally monolingual. Furthermore, beginning with the 1960s, the phenomenon of mass tourism brought with it a new wave of outsiders, totally ignorant of Catalan national life and only concerned with the emptiest clichés of Spanish folklore, clichés which Franco's regime skilfully exploited.

It was not a revolt that put an end to the dictatorship but the physical decease of Franco in his bed. The regime was gently liquidated, without major disruption, but through compromise and transition instead. Although Catalan democrats had played an important role in the resistance to Franco's regime, their representatives had to be content, in the Spanish constitution of 1978 and the statute for Catalan autonomy of 1979, with legal documents which, as far as language was concerned, formalised the disadvantages suffered by Catalan compared to Spanish. Knowledge of the latter is a duty, while knowledge of the former is merely a right which, consequentially, anyone who wishes to can cheerfully renounce. The law of 1983, promulgating linguistic 'normalisation' for Catalunya, could hardly do more than spell out the implications of both the constitution and the statute. Sanctions were excluded. The only course open was to ensure that the public use of Catalan was not penalised (no-one was to be prosecuted for using the language either in private or in public), while reaffirming the undeniable presence in Catalonia (now given 'democratic' legitimacy) of a language, Spanish, which had been introduced by brute force, that is, with blood and flames.

And so, under conditions of formal democracy, Catalan society continues to be overwhelmingly Spanish-speaking in such crucial areas as the law, business and the mass media – omnipotent and omnipresent. In this last field, with the early 1980s, the autonomous Catalan government or *Generalitat* set up Catalan language media, which can do little more than palliate the serious deficit of radio and television broadcasting in Catalan.

In the area of compulsory education, not directly subject to the inflexible laws of the capitalist market (always tending to favour the silent majority as against smaller groups) the *Generalitat* resisted the initial temptation to set up a parallel network of separate teaching in two languages and instead introduced a policy of 'language immersion' within a single system, which aims to render all children fluent in Catalan, the language of their country. These energetic measures on the part of the autonomous government have, however, proved totally incapable of bringing about the 'linguistic normalisation' mentioned above, were this only in the sense of giving Catalan a status equal to that of Spanish, where everyday use in Catalan life is concerned.

Moreover, the policy of 'language immersion' has provoked the anger of Spanish colonialists, totally opposed to abandoning the dominant role their language has enjoyed for centuries, in schools and elsewhere. For some years now they have been pursuing, through certain political parties and various media, and through particularly active groups of Spanish-speaking immigrants cast in the role of a Trojan horse, a campaign which denigrates the language policies of the *Generalitat*. Their objective is, yet again, to reduce Catalan to the position of a tribal idiom, used only in emotional and family contexts by a remnant of speakers. Were they to succeed, then Spanish rather than Catalan would be the unifying factor, fusing together in one single melting-pot the diverse strands of contemporary Catalan society.

Spanish colonialism is intrinsically hostile to Catalan and it is hardly surprising that it should also attack the unity of the language. Since the beginning of the last century, for the historical reasons outlined above, the Principality (Catalonia in the strictest sense) has formed the core of a group of territories, never completely integrated and known as the Catalan lands or *Països Catalans*, which have in common only a language and a culture. Each of the lands has a different history and this has weakened awareness of their original shared identity. As a result, both the Valencia region and the Balearic Islands are being increasingly assimilated to Spain, while Northern Catalonia is assimilated to France – the victim of an institutionalised Jacobinism which continues today implacably to proscribe any public manifestation of the area's indigenous language.

In this context, and with the help of statutes of autonomy which are deliberately ambiguous where language is concerned, Spanish colonialists have turned to the old strategy of 'divide and rule', fostering separatist local sentiment, opposed to both Catalonia and Spain, and claiming that a distinctive language exists for Valencia (or for Mallorca, or Minorca, or Ibiza), totally different from the shared language which is known internationally under the generic name of Catalan. At the time of writing, the autonomous government of the Valencia region is in the hands of parties representing the Spanish right wing and folkloristic provincialism, who have gone so far as to concoct a spurious, aberrant grammar in order to fan the flames of linguistic separatism, ignoring any of the scientific criteria revelation to the codification of a natural language.

Manoeuvres of this kind cannot, however, alter the effective unity of Catalan, or the validity of Fabra's proposals for standardisation, supported both by writers and, in the last analysis, by all educated speakers of the language in the Valencia region (where, indeed, the only weekly news magazine embracing all the Catalan lands to appear so far, *El Temps,* is published) and in the Balearic Islands. At the same time they undeniably confuse the mass of Catalan speakers in these areas, whose sense of national identity has already been weakened, and by doing so foment their progressive assimilation to Spain, from the grass roots upwards.

The phenomenon of Spanish replacing Catalan is currently more widespread among the lower classes than among the others, just as the informal registers of Catalan are those most strongly affected by interference from Spanish. We are therefore witnesses to the reversal of a tendency, dating as far back as the 16th century, to relegate Catalan to domestic and colloquial use. It is now, in contrast, a language of culture perfectly suited to meet all the expressive requirements of the contemporary world with its complex and dynamic historical realities. It can boast normally functioning written and audiovisual media, notwithstanding the powerful competition caused by massive immigration from the rest of Spain. Its output, in terms of literature and publishing, can measure up to the challenges of the parallel output in Spanish, and has created a public which can at least ensure its survival. Catalonia has several universities, where teaching is to all effects equally split between the two languages.

But this means that, more than ever before, Catalan runs the risk of turning into a species of Latin, used liturgically for elevated purposes. Within Catalan society today, it is above all Spanish which distinguishes people from one another and therefore, inevitably, offers the possibility of integration, a function assumed first and foremost by language in modern societies. The mechanisms regulating promotion or blockage in terms of class operate primarily in Spanish. Catalan is of secondary importance where access to the job market is concerned, and there are even activities where it is more crucial to know English than to know Catalan.

There again, increasing interference from Spanish language mass media and from the Spanish speaking population settled in Catalonia effectively undermines the achievements of compulsory schooling, literature and publishing in fostering the Catalan language and disseminating Catalan culture among those who speak it. The latter are losing their linguistic competence, more and more ignorant of basic and genuine elements, which are discarded in favour of unnecessary loans from Spanish. It hardly needs pointing out that this tendency is clearest in the city of Barcelona. This is all the more worrying, since the major innovations (including the replacement of one language by another), to which no language is immune, usually spread outwards from the capital, which has unquestionable superiority in terms of population, social influence and power.

It is not easy to predict what the future of Catalan will be. All one can say is that the years immediately ahead of us, with the end of this century and the arrival of the millennium, will be crucial in deciding whether the language is consolidated in full and normal use within Catalan society, or is replaced by Spanish in a fashion that could be very rapid indeed.

At present there can be no denying that all the measures undertaken by the institutions of both the autonomous and the local administrations and within civil society, with the intention of normalising the status of the language, have proved frankly insufficient. It is true that minimal progress has been made in spreading the active use of Catalan among the Spanish-speaking population, and that there have been significant advances in introducing Catalan into areas which proved resolutely refractory until now, such as the judiciary and the business world. But there has proved to be no way of inducing Catalans to carry on speaking their own tongue when faced with a Spanish speaker who presumably understands it, and thereby practising what is known as passive bilingualism. Nor has it been possible to convince them that they have every legal right, within the territory of Catalonia, to insist on using the language of that territory in any circumstances whatsoever, be they public or private.

Currently applicable legal procedures give Spanish an unfair advantage over Catalan, and the Catalan *Generalitat* (like the autonomous governments of the other Catalan lands, the Balearic Islands and the Valencia region, it goes without saying) pursues a language policy based merely on compromise. A considerable sector of Catalan society shows less and less interest in the language of the country they were either born in or emigrated to. According to the pithy conclusions of Albert Branchadell, in a recent analysis of the process of linguistic normalisation, these are the principal stumbling blocks facing any attempt to ensure for Catalan a comparable status in its own society to that of any other language of culture with a similar number of speakers, inside its own historical territory.

There can be no question at present of major changes to either the Spanish Constitution or the Statute of Autonomy. The way to correct the reigning imbalance would be to reform the current legal provisions for Linguistic Normalisation (the *Llei de Normalització Lingüística*) so as to bring about genuine changes in the world of business and in the judiciary. Catalan would then achieve genuine prestige within the mechanisms of legal and economic power and, as a result, become increasingly essential to the functioning of such crucial areas of any society.

What is more, such a legal reform would have to be indissolubly linked to a social programme which saw Catalan as a valid means of self-promotion, rather than as a species to be saved from extinction, bringing the appropriate pressure to bear on all political parties, be they left or right, in favour of independence, nationalist-inspired or led from Madrid. That way they would fight, at the very least, for Catalan to reach genuine

and effective equality with Spanish in that lands that historically consti-
tuted Catalonia.

Leaving aside the indubitable difficulties inherent in such policies,
scholars and people active in culture, as well as those citizens most sen-
sitised to the issue, are unanimous in declaring that the fate of Catalan will
be freely decided by those who speak it. In the developed world at any
rate, society seems to have left behind the ghost of any kind of totalitar-
ianism and to have made a definite commitment to regimes which protect
the formal liberties of every citizen. Even a strongly centralised state,
determined to protect and foster a language, could not do so if its citizens,
for whatever reason, chose to abandon it and adopt a different one.

And yet, given that throughout history the people of Catalonia have
shown a constant determination to affirm their own existence, one may
hope that, yet again, a majority of people in the stateless nation which has
the most lively and powerful language of all Europe's stateless nations will
once more choose to remain faithful to their age-old tongue, rendering it
worthy to take its justified place within the ample and varied assembly of
nations of the world.

Maria-Mercè Marçal

From *Sister Stranger*

Flesh, without words,
in front of me and in me.

Me, who had read all the books.

La carn, sense paraules,
davant de mi i en mi.

I jo que havia llegit tots els llibres.

*

He is there. And I am. Mingling in a face
exposed for the first time to thirteen winds
                    patched up with new rain ...
And we are not. Scissors have torn the root.
Frayed knots. And a door broken open.

I trace the whole way back upstream in vain.
All the hawsers have been cut. The waters are undone.
The boats which tried to pass a bridge are shattered.
And, in spite of it all, confused in a face, he and I.

And we are not. A new froth blossoms on the strait
that joins and separates: who knows where the source is?
Lowering its nets into these waters, life takes what
belongs to it, forgetting who he is, who I am,
what kind of love cast old dice at the meeting point,
what chance set chance afire, spark in the wood:
the contours of the leaves bury it all.

Hi és ell. I jo. Barrejats en un rostre
que estrena els tretze vents
                    sargits amb pluja nova ...
no hi som. Les tisores han destrossat l'arrel.
Nusos ratats. I una porta esbotzada.

Riu amunt ressegueixo en va tots els topants.
Tots els llibants trencats, les aigües desnuades.
Estellades les barques que intentaven un pont.
I, malgrat tot, confosos en un rostre, ell i jo.

I no hi som. És el freu que uneix i que separa
florit d'escuma nova: qui sap on és la deu?
La vida que ha calat xarxes en aquest tram
pren el que és seu i oblida qui és ell, qui sóc jo,
quin amor ha llançat daus vells a l'enforcall
i quin atzar va encendre l'atzar, d'espurna a bosc:
Tot ho colga el relleu continu de les fulles.

*

Car si près que tu sois l'air circule entre nous.
M. Desbordes-Valmore

Ivy,
        martial victory,
                sister,
stranger, all at once become a presence:
How can I decipher your barbaric,
violent language forcing my frontiers
and drawing blood, a challenge I cannot
even use my legs to escape from!
What eyes, what hands – surely not mine – would be
capable of seeing you as only touch,
as beauty made flesh, disclosed upon my belly,
no questions asked? I cannot stop myself
longing for the ears that strained to catch
your voice, when you were nothing but the shadow
of a murmur of high leaves inside my body,
desire, smoke signals that traversed the wood
from one side to the other, sound of drums,
open, far off, a dove with a white beak
where I inscribed, using an alphabet
of plants, your message, living poem that
did not demand an answer like the one
I now know I don't have. And, nonetheless,
victory is the name that I bestow
upon you, martial ivy, sister, stranger.

Car si près que tu sois l'air circule entre nous.
M. Desbordes-Valmore

Heura,
        victòria marçal,
                germana
estrangera, de cop feta present:
Com desxifrar el teu llenguatge bàrbar
i violent que força els meus confins
fins a la sang, un repte que no em deixa

ni les cames tan sols per a fugir!
¿Quins ulls i quines mans – no pas les meves –
sabrien veure't com un tacte, sols,
com la bellesa feta carn, desclosa
sobre el meu ventre, sense interrogants?
No puc deixar d'enyorar les orelles
endevines que et caçaven la veu
quan només eres l'ombra d'un murmuri
de fulles altes, cos endins, desig,
senyals de fum de l'una a l'altra banda
del bosc, so de tabals, obert, llunyà,
colom amb bec en blanc, on jo inscrivia
l'alfabet vegetal del teu missatge,
poema viu que no urgia resposta
com ara aquesta que sé que no sé.
I malgrat tot t'anomeno victòria,
heura marçal, germana, l'estrangera.

*

For you, I would like
to take the road to Lilliput,
my saddle-bags full
of lawless songs,
and reach the field
where chance is a king
without any clothes
who'll sell his sword
to vice or to virtue.

Per tu voldria anar
camí de Lilliput
amb les alforgues plenes
de cançons sense llei,
i trobar-nos al prat
on l'atzar és un rei
despullat, franc d'espasa,
de vici, de virtut.

*

Two teeth have left
the mark of a pomegranate
on my breast, when you still don't
have them to sink
into what melts for you.

Dues dents han deixat
un rastre de magrana
al meu pit, quan encara
tu no en tens per clavar-les
en allò que se't fon.

*

This pleasure that draws blood
will hurl me from the precipice.
With all my strength I grip
the words that allow me
to continue
mounting the rope.

Aquest plaer sagnant
vol estimbar-me.
M'aferro amb força
a les paraules
que em permeten seguir
dalt la maroma.

*

What is the toothless sun
that smiles at me from a world
I knew long, long ago
and have forgotten?
Wild birds have eaten the crumbs
left to mark my path.

¿Quin sol desdentegat
em somriu des d'un món
que vaig conèixer fa
molt temps i que he oblidat?
Ocells salvatges s'han menjat les molles
que vaig anar deixant per fer camí.

*

Who dictates the words I speak to you,
encrusting me with grimaces and gestures?
Who speaks and moves in me? It's the Impostor,
the one who lived in me without my knowing
until you came. That is when She emerged,
like a shadow, from uncharted attics,
possessing me like a tyrannic lover,
moving me like a puppet at a fair.
I can often see her in the mirror,
ransomed from I cannot tell what ashes.
It doesn't bother you when She speaks to you,
even if She steals my voice and face.
If, with her amorous and brutal body,
She should bar the door of exit for you,
then you must kill her and feel no remorse.
Do it for me as well, and in my name:
She is too far inside me for my step
to halt on the threshold of suicide.

Qui em dicta les paraules quan et parlo?
Qui m'incrusta de gestos i ganyotes?
Qui parla i fa per mi? És la Impostora.
M'habitava sense que jo ho sabés
fins que vingueres. Llavors va sorgir
de no sé quines golfes, com una ombra,
i em posseeix com un amant tirànic
i em mou com el titella d'una fira.
I sovint, al mirall, la veig a Ella
rescatada de no sé quina cendra.
No li facis cap cas quan Ella et parla,
encara que m'usurpi veu i rostre.
I si et barra la porta de sortida
amb el seu cos amorós i brutal
cal que la matis sense cap recança.
Fes-ho per mi també i en el meu nom:
Jo la tinc massa endins i no sabria
aturar-me al llindar del suïcidi.

Between Twelve and One

Quim Monzó

The man draws on his cigarette and picks up the receiver. "Hello?"

"Hi there." A woman is speaking. "It's me."

The man straightens up. He stubs out the cigarette in the ashtray next to the telephone. He speaks in a low voice: "I've told you a thousand times never to call me at home."

"The thing is ... "

"I've told you always to call me at the office."

"Can you talk?"

"Obviously not. Can't you tell?"

"Where is ... she?"

"Next door."

"Can she hear us ... hear you?"

"No. But she could come in at any moment."

"Forgive me. I'm sorry. But I had to call you now. I couldn't wait till you were at work tomorrow."

A silence follows. The man breaks it. "Why?"

"Because this situation causes me a lot of pain."

"What situation?"

"Ours. Who else's?"

"Well ... We can sort it out ... "

"No! No. Don't say a thing. There's no point." She is trying to be ironic and making a mess of it. "She might hear you."

"She can't hear me, now. Listen ... "

"I think the time has come to make a decision."

"What decision?"

"Can't you imagine?"

"I'm not in the mood for guessing games, Maria."

"I have to choose. Between you and him."

"And?"

"And, since you can't give me everything I want ... Let's not kid ourselves: for you, I'll never be anything more than ... " She breathes deeply. An ambulance can be heard passing, far off. "You don't want to leave her, do you? I don't even know why I ask. I already know the answer."

"What's all that noise?"

"I'm calling from a phone box."

"We've been through this a thousand times. I've always been sincere with you. I've never lied about how things are. We suit each other, don't we? That means ... "

"But I'm really in love with you. And I already know you aren't a bit in love with me."

"I've always said I don't want to hurt you in any way. I've never promised you anything. Have I ever promised you anything?"

"No."

"You have to decide what we do."

"Yes."

"Isn't that what I've always told you? That you have to decide?"

"Yes. That's why I called. Because my decision's already taken."

"I've always played by the rules, with you." He stops. "What's your decision?"

"I've decided … not to see you any longer." The woman says it and bursts into tears. She cries for quite a while. Little by little, the sobs grow gentler. The man takes the opportunity to talk.

"I'm sorry, but if that is really what … " The woman breaks in:

"But don't you realise that I don't want to stop seeing you?"

When the sound of tears has stopped, the man says: "Maria … "

"No." She wipes her eyes. "I'd rather you didn't say anything."

All at once, the man raises his voice: "Actually, it'd make more sense to pick a car that gives you a better performance."

"What?"

"Especially if you're talking about that kind of mileage." He stops for a moment. "Yes." Another pause. "Yes, I understand. Obviously I can't give you any advice on that point. But my impression is you'd be better off with a car that gives much more … much more … " He appears to be looking for a word. "Yes, I agree. But it uses too much petrol."

"Can't you talk?"

"Of course I can't."

"Is she close by?"

"Yes."

"In front of you?"

"Yes. But the price of that model isn't so very different from the Japanese ones. And the Japanese … "

"Your wife is standing in front of you and here I am, with no idea what to do." She gets more and more indignant. "Unable to decide once and for all to put an end to this nonsense."

"Four doors would be ideal. What you want is four doors."

"Don't you see there's no other solution? We can't go on like this. We can't even have a civilized conversation."

"But that one consumes six and a half litres."

"You are talking about cars, petrol consumption, four doors or two, and I can't even find the strength to hang up."

"Just a moment." The man has put his hand over the receiver. The woman can hear muffled voices. "She says … " Hand over the receiver again. "Anna wants you to tell Lluisa that the cake turned out perfectly."

"Who do you think you're talking to?"

"Fine then, we'll meet up."

"Do you want me to hang up or … ? Tell me before ending if we can meet tomorrow."

"Yes."

"There's no way out. I ring to tell you it's finished and end up asking you if tomorrow ... Same place as usual?"

"Yes."

"Same time as usual?"

"Exactly."

"And" – her voice has gone soft – "will we do the usual things? I can see you on your knees in front of me, lifting my skirt ... Will you lick me? Bite me? Will you really hurt me?"

"Ye-es." His voice drops again. "For God's sake, Maria. She nearly realised. She's in the kitchen now but she could come back any minute. What would have happened if she'd asked me to put you on to her?"

"Why should she want to speak to me?"

"I don't mean you. I mean the person she thought I was speaking to."

"There's no way to understand you. And I'm the same. I just can't take any more, I decide to end it and, the minute I hear your voice, all my decisions go up in smoke. I'd love to be with you now. Why not come? You can't? Obviously not. It doesn't matter. It's when I can't speak to you I can't cope. Do you love me?"

"Of course I do."

"We'd better hang up. Goodbye."

"Where are you?"

"In a bar. I already told you."

"No. You told me you were in a phone box."

"If you knew I was in a phone box, why did you ask me again?"

"But you aren't in a phone box, you're in a bar. At any rate, that's what you're telling me now."

"A bar, a phone box. What difference does it make?"

"'What difference', 'What difference' ... "

"Look, I've had enough!"

"What are you planning to do now?"

"Now? About us, you mean?"

"No. I mean right now. Are you thinking of going to the cinema? Have you had lunch? Have you got an acting class?"

"Look, I'm going to hang up."

"Wait a minute."

"The thing is ... "

"Sometimes, Maria, I think that, if we wanted to, if only we really set our minds to it, we could arrange things differently, without all this hassle."

"Yes, I suppose we could."

"Could what?"

"Yes."

"What's going on? Can't you talk? Is someone there? Is that why you can't talk?"

"Hmm ... Yes."

"You arranged to meet him in the bar and he's there now. Or he was already with you and now he's come to the phone. Yes or no? Or what else?"

"I'll give you back the book. Stop worrying."

"I'm not one of your woman friends."

"Cheers then. Call me. And remember I'll give you back the book."

"Oh no. Don't hang up now! I've had to put up with listening to you and not being able to answer anything but rubbish and now … "

"I haven't heard of that one. What did you say the title was?"

"Perfect. You do that so well. Now you'll tell me the title. Won't you?"

"Yes … "

"Spot on, the 'yes'. It makes it convincing, makes the dialogue with the girl you're supposed to be talking to seem real."

"*Love in the Afternoon,* is that what it's called?"

"Is that a hint, an invitation?"

"But *A Hundred Crosses* was much better than *Love in the Afternoon.* As far as I'm concerned, at any rate."

"I haven't read that one, you know. Is it a novel too?"

"*A Hundred Crosses?* Boring?"

Suddenly the man's voice is serious again: "But I've already explained. It consumes much less petrol than the other one."

"But I find the heroine of *Love in the Afternoon* more convincing."

"And why didn't a firm like Peugeot think of a gearbox like that?"

"But wasn't that *Now We Two Are Equals.* Or am I getting mixed up?"

"Absolutely."

"And so?"

"Nothing."

There is a short pause.

"Can't you see there's nothing to be done? Now I can talk properly again." Yet another pause. "Haven't you got anything to say? Have you finished chatting, or do you want to leave off cars and move onto something else?"

"I'm alone again too."

"Goodbye then."

"You're right. The best thing we can do is say goodbye."

"I have something to tell you first."

"Go ahead."

"I'm pregnant." He doesn't answer.

"Do you hear me? I'm pregnant. By you."

"How can it be me? How do you know it's me?"

"Because I've only been with you since I had my last period, nutcase!"

"And this guy who can give you everything I can't? Haven't you … ? Sorry. What are you going to do?"

"What do you mean, what am I going to do? Don't you have anything to say about it?"

"Me? No."

"Well then. Now I really see the kind of man you are. Now I realise that, if I were ever to be in that situation, you wouldn't take the slightest interest."

"What do you mean 'if I were ever to be in that situation'?"

"It obviously means I'm not pregnant. Do you take me for a fool? I just had the idea, to find out how you would react in a situation like that. Do you believe that if I were really pregnant I'd have asked you what to do or what not to do?"

His voice is angry: "Listen, Maria … !"

She challenges him: "What? What do you want me to listen to?"

"You know I won't have you speaking to me like that, in that tone of voice, defying me!"

"Really?"

"I'll smash your face!"

"Will you now?"

"I'll punch your face till your eyes swell up."

"Yes … "

"Till you shriek."

"Yes … "

"I'll tie you to the bedposts."

"Yes, yes … "

"I'll spit in your mouth."

"Yes!"

"I'll slap your face till it bleeds."

"Yes, yes!"

"I'll force you to … "

"To what? To what?"

"I'll fill your mouth with it. And I'll force you to swallow the whole lot: you won't let even a drop escape."

"Not one."

The woman's breathing is agitated. The man is excited. "Not one, I said! Lick up the drop that's trickling along your lower lip."

"'Pig', call me a 'pig' … "

"Pig. Kneel down and open your mouth."

The woman gasps. "That's enough. I have to tell you whatever the consequences. It's crazy trying to drag it out any longer." She is silent for a moment, as if to gather courage. "Listen: I'm not Maria."

"What do you mean, you're not Maria?"

"I'm not Maria: that's what I mean. Maria is … Maria asked me to phone you up and talk as if I was her."

"You're taking me for a ride."

"She had to leave. And she wanted … "

"To leave for where?"

"Somewhere outside the city. She wanted you to think she was here and not … The thing is … I can't go on pretending something that isn't true. Look: Maria and I know each other from acting classes. I study at drama school too. She asked me to call you and arrange things so we argued. Because you're supposed to be seeing each other tomorrow and she won't be back in time. Are you listening?"

"Where is she?"

"She's gone away for a week. With a man."

"With whom?"

"Jaume."

"With Jaume?"

"Yes."

"Which Jaume?"

"Jaume Ibarra."

"But listen: I'm Jaume Ibarra. Who did you think you were talking to? What number did you call?"

"You're Jaume?"

"Yes."

"Good God."

"Who did you think you were talking to?"

"Joan[1]."

"To Joan? You mean, Maria and Joan ... "

"Now I get it: I dialled the wrong number."

"And how come you've got my number?"

"Maria wrote them both down for me, one above the other, and I got it wrong: I dialled the wrong one."

"Why did you take down my number if you weren't supposed to phone me? Or was I someone else you had to phone? But then you said you thought she had gone off with me ... "

"If I told you the truth, you wouldn't believe me."

"Hey, tell me something ... What's your name?"

"Carme."

"Carme, tell me ... "

The woman cuts him short. "Just a minute. Are you really Jaume? But Jaume doesn't live with anybody! It's Joan that lives with his wife. Why did you tell me your wife was standing in front of you?"

"You are hardly truth incarnate either."

"If you thought you were talking to Maria, why did you try and convince me you lived with a woman?"

"Well, we do that sort of thing, Maria and I, now and again. Hardly at all more recently, believe me, just now and again. As a game."

"She never told me."

"Why should she have told you? Do you tell each other everything?"

"More or less."

"Really? What does she tell you about me?"

"Hmm."

"What do you mean, 'hmm'?"

"I mean she tells me all the interesting bits."

"Down to the smallest details?"

"Down to the smallest details, leaving nothing out."

"Where are you?"

"In a bar, I already told you."

"You also said you were in a phone box."

"Cut it with this phone box!"

"What are you doing now?"

---

1. A *man's* name, the Catalan form of "John", pronounced "Zhwan".

"You already asked me that."

"Then you were Maria. Maybe now you're Carme your plans are different. And then, when you were Maria you refused to answer too."

The man bites his lip. "Why don't we meet up?"

"When?"

"Today?"

"It'd have to be this evening. I have a class this afternoon."

"This evening then."

"Where?"

"The bar at the Ritz?"

"OK."

"At eight o'clock?"

"At eight o'clock I get out of class. Let's say half past."

"How will I recognise you?"

"I'll be wearing a leather jacket, the one you gave her a month before... I'll be wearing a leather jacket."

"A month before what?" The woman is silent. "The jacket: I gave her it a month before what?"

"I have to tell you, Jaume. Otherwise I'll burst."

"Tell me then."

"Maria is dead. You gave her the jacket a month before she died. Listen ... I shouldn't ... I know how much you loved each other. And when she died I decided, the whole class decided together ... "

"I find this joke in very bad taste."

"Let's meet up and talk. At half past eight. OK? Or, if you want, I can miss the class."

"I saw her last week."

"She's been dead for five months."

"I've seen her time and again over the last five months. I was with her last week. She was very alive, very beautiful. She wasn't some sort of a ghost."

"For five months you've been going out with a Maria who isn't Maria."

"And according to you, who's been acting Maria all this time?"

"Me."

"I'd have noticed."

"I'm telling you the truth."

"If that were so, what would make you decide you didn't want to meet up with me tomorrow?"

"I'm fed up pretending to be Maria."

"Far from it. You just agreed that we would meet."

"Because now I'll be Carme, not Maria. Please, Jaume, I'll explain it to you later."

"And how come you didn't realise I was Jaume and not Joan?"

"Do you think I didn't know who I was calling? I had no doubt you were Jaume. I know you perfectly well. I've been seeing you for five months. And five months means a lot. Even enough to know that ... " (the woman's voice breaks) "I've fallen madly in love with you. And I want to put an end to this farce."

"I don't believe a single word of all this. How could you have managed to stop me noticing, all these times we've met (according to you, that is), that you weren't Maria?"

"Don't forget I go to drama school."

"What the hell does your drama school matter? How do you imagine I can believe I wouldn't have noticed the difference? All I need now is for you to come out with the old chestnut about twin sisters ... But listen, Maria has, she had, a twin sister."

"That's me."

"I've never seen her."

"You've seen her often enough. That is, all the times you've seen me! A couple of times each week for the last five months. Some weeks once only: that's what we need to talk about. Because I want to see you more often. Shall we meet as we agreed? At half past eight?"

"And your name is really Carme?"

"At half past eight? OK?"

"Yes."

"I do love you. If I ever stopped loving you, I'd die."

Illustration by Alfons Bytautas

Normality and the Catalan Woman Writer

Neus Real

In the spring of last year I was asked to give a talk about women's writing, in connection with the launching of a new magazine featuring Catalan literature and thought. It seemed appropriate to take a general approach. Nevertheless, I had a precise starting point (though there was no need to make it explicit). On the one hand was my (at least) threefold stance as a Catalan woman, fledgling literary scholar and co-editor of a section of the magazine. On the other, my overall enthusiasm for literature and my special interest in women's writing and, more specifically, Catalan women's writing. The main focus of what I said then, and of the ideas prompted by a round table on the same topic (again connected with the magazine) and the discussions with a range of people that followed, was how much the issue matters today and what is the best stance to approach it from. In this essay I want to formulate these questions and take them a little further. My purpose is to articulate a vague cluster of ideas at the root of which is a desire to have women's writing in general, and the writing of Catalan women in particular, treated as normal. At the same time I want to offer a broad outline of Catalan women's writing since the middle of the last century. Limitations of space will force me to leave out many names and to aim at the utmost concision, staying very much on the surface. And yet it is still worth attempting the briefest of sketches.

Not long ago a friend of mine, a writer from Galicia in north west Spain, told me a curious story of a book about a criminal trial, written by another Galician before the Spanish Civil War. Galician scholars and critics had, without exception, read the text in nationalist terms: the accused person stood for Galicia, while the judge, and the whole legal apparatus, represented the oppressive power of Spain. A Galician specialist from an English university (if I am not mistaken, in a paper for an academic congress) offered a reading that nobody had thought of until then. He saw it merely as the account of how a guilty man tries to evade the punishment the law imposes on him. The English academic had approached the Galician text as he would have done any work of literature. He did not view it as primarily polemical or nationalistic. And the greatest beneficiary of this new perspective was, of course, the text itself. The new reading underlined the richness of the book, its possibilities as a literary creation and the impossibility of confining and thereby impoverishing it (which is always a form of oppression).

This incident, drawn from real life, shows what can happen when institutions impose particular ways of reading literary texts. In this specific case, the filter applied was Galician nationalism, and the result a single way of reading (therein lies the problem). Yet the book offered other possibilities, which Galician scholars and critics (according to my friend) only started to explore after the agreeable surprise of the English academic's contribution.

There are countless filters of this kind, and no doubt it is hard to become conscious of them and control their limiting influence. But maybe the most inspiring and enriching results are the consequence of approaching texts, not within determined schemes such as nationalism, gender, race, social class and so on, but from normality rather than from marginality. The normality I am talking about does not occlude difference and diversity. It means approaching any literary text without preconceptions. In the case of women's writing this would remove the obligation to speak of its otherness, its marginality or strangeness within the patriarchal society where it has been and continues to be produced. During a particular stage of feminist studies the older approach, which has an undeniable historical justification, led to useful and stimulating results. Today, however, even when it aims to revalue and to champion women's writing, it all too often supports what it claims to be fighting. Circumstances have changed and feminist theory has evolved. Despite the strong case that can be made against the word, given its ideological colouring within western patriarchal culture (where the norm is the rule imposed by men in positions of power), to call women's writing 'normal' is to reject the 'abnormality' that has traditionally dogged it, given historical domination by men's culture. In the last decade of the 20th century, appropriating such a central concept, from what has been historically a marginal position in that culture, can have much more radical consequences, as against insistence on a marginality which nowadays seems rather dubious. Just think of the important changes brought about by the struggle to free women in every area of life, and not only literature!

There is no question that women have gradually gained their own space in public life since the 19th century, with the First World War and the 1960s as crucial stages in the process. As far as Catalan culture and literature are concerned, the launching in the 1880s of a cultural renaissance, based on a strongly nationalist ideology, coincided with the hesitant beginnings of the feminist movement, albeit on very different bases than in the countries where it originated. The two battles were, however, distinct, even if they occurred at the same time. If Catalan women writers then, such as Maria Domènech, Carme Karr, Dolors Monserdà (who asked her husband's permission before publishing), Maria Antonia Salvà, Palmira Ventós and others, chose to write in Catalan, notwithstanding the prevailing political and cultural conditions, they were not only making a 'nationalist' statement but also, as they moved into the public sphere, and in the specific characteristics of their books, adopting a political compromise as women. This is a very complex issue, which must be seen in the appropriate historical and cultural perspective, with its own nuances and particular circumstances.

The process they began was one of the factors which made it possible for a novel of the stature of *Solitude* to appear at the beginning of the present century, written by Caterina Albert i Paradís (who used the pseudonym 'Victor Català'), by general agreement a canonical text in Catalan literature. It also laid the basis, along with other factors, for the emergence of a numerous group of young women writers in the 1920s and 30s: Rosa Maria Arquimbau, Aurora Bertrana, Elvira Augusta Lewi, Carme Montoriol,

Anna Murià, Maria Verger and Maria Teresa Vernet, among others. Most of them fell silent after the Spanish Civil War, whose severe consequences for Catalan culture are well known. Yet later, when the war was over, one of them, Mercè Rodoreda, was to produce a body of writing which gained notable recognition for its literary merit in both Europe and North America.

Her fiction appeared at the same time as that of Maria Aurèlia Capmany and other women writers. The political and cultural changes accompanying the final years of Franco's dictatorship gave a strong impulse to feminism and to Catalan culture, both strongly opposed to the authoritarian regime. A group of writers including Maria Mercè Marçal, Carme Riera, Montserrat Roig and Isabel-Clara Simó, for all the difficulties they faced, and the ups and downs in the contemporary world of Catalan literature and culture, were able to look back upon a past and a tradition as Catalan women writers. The same goes for those who began publishing in the 1980s, such as Maria Barbal, and younger writers such as Maria de la Pau Janer. People have spoken of three generations of Catalan women writers since the 19th century (and, if it is worth speaking in such terms, it would be better to envisage four). Each has its own cultural setting, with specific, concrete features, appertaining to Catalan literature in the first place and, secondly, to Catalan culture in general.

Women in general, and specifically Catalan women writers, have a history of their own, and one which is public as well as private. That history has today become fashionable. If issues around women and women's literature have become so topical throughout the western world (and Catalonia is no exception here) then, to a certain extent at least, the silence about women's history which traditional feminists denounced has at last been broken. Several factors prove this to be the case, in a general sense. We are nowadays familiar with discussions about the 'feminisation' of attitudes, approaches and behaviour and the so-called 'undermining' of men in all areas of society. This applies both to theoretical consideration by academics and the practical world of business, to mention two extremes. As regards 'feminisation', I am thinking in particular of certain tendencies in philosophy which have used the term to work out a new system of thought, as with Jacques Derrida and his followers. There can be no ignoring the proliferation of debate, on television and in newspapers, supplements and magazines, and published studies, about women and power, women and literature, and similar topics. And of course one cannot forget the achievements of feminism, and all the initiatives and activities undertaken by feminists, in a range of different forms.

Turning specifically to Catalan literature and culture, at any rate in Barcelona itself, there can be no denying the topicality of women's writing, even if this is to a lesser extent the case than in other cultures, such as those of France or England. All one has to do, to see the most obvious evidence, is wander down the street and glance at the newsstalls and bookshops, noticing how many books by women are on sale, biographies of women artists and writers and writers' wives, collections of letters, works by Catalan women writers, translations of the work of women writers from abroad ... (It is worth pointing out that there are many more books on sale in Spanish than in Catalan, except in the field of Catalan literature. But that leads into another order of problems, connected with marketing, which cannot be entered into here.) At another level, for some years now, specific studies of Catalan women writers have begun to appear. Besides individual publishing schemes, which have made available texts only to be traced in a library or two before, there are already books and articles about the history of our women writers, although a great deal remains to be done.

The active presence of women writers and of the literature written by them and about them (in Catalan and many other languages), as well as its quality and its importance on the contemporary scene, after many years of battling and effort, are undeniable to anyone who follows the processes and products of cultural life with a minimum of assiduity. Feminist criticism in particular, with determined insistence, has committed itself to demonstrating this fact, and continues to do so. The very existence of such critical approaches is, at least in one sense, a response to this presence, since from its very beginnings they have concentrated on literary texts written by women. What makes it so exciting is that, in the most recent theoretical discussions, part of what is known as the second wave of feminism, feminist criticism has set about revising its basic assumptions in the light of a range of problems. All I can do here is to simplify overwhelmingly a series of complex considerations, part of the large scale development of a school of thought which is both heterogeneous and multiple. Nevertheless, without pulling the wool over anybody's eyes, I think I can underline one fundamental feature: discussions about the dangers of self-marginalisation, of giving legitimacy to forms of behaviour which are opposed to the basic historical aims of feminism.

I see this as a major warning signal from those working with theory. Because they realise the difficulties and the implications of declaring the existence of a 'feminine' literature, for example, theoreticians have had to revise an idea so instrumental and useful to feminists politics as that of gender. Accepting the idea of gender brought with it problems of concept, method and ideology which tended to reproduce the annihilation of difference, by throwing together very distinct realities under terms like 'woman' or 'feminine'. The term 'gender' had to be reconsidered. A subjectivity that was multiple, diverse and multifaceted had to be conceptualised, on where sex and its cultural representation are important, but where both can appear, represent and take shape in a multiplicity of forms, together with all their constituent elements (race, nationality, social class, cultural environment, experience and so on). In the light of this reconsideration, it seems impossible to carry on using a series of binary oppositions (man/woman, subject/object, oppressor/oppressed etc.). These had a historical usefulness but can no longer help bring about the transformation which we seek.

Where Catalan women writers are concerned, as with women writers from other so-called 'minority' cultures, this system of oppositions took shape along two major trajectories, based on the idea of oppression. The reference to their (at the very least) doubly oppressed condition is inevitable: as women in Catalan society and culture (compared to men) and, politically and culturally, as Catalans within a Spanish state (compared to Spaniards). I am, however, more interested in the first trajectory, especially where it concerns the historical definition of our culture. A characteristic feature of the way Catalan culture has been talked about since the 19th century is the repeated negative use of the term 'normal', in various guises, taking the major European cultures as points of comparison. Cultural 'normality' was what Catalans aimed essentially to achieve, as against a supposedly 'abnormal' reality, and the evidence would seem to indicate that they are still some distance away from it.

Logically, Catalan women writers would have to be viewed as doubly 'abnormal', if we apply this paradigm of marginality within the usual scheme of oppositions. But one has the suspicion that, even if the current situation bears out the reality of political and cultural oppression in both senses (from Spain and from patriarchy), the people who contribute to this abnormality are those who insist on talking about it and thereby making it a reality. Seen from this point of view, the major responsibility for the perceived abnormality, in general, of Catalan culture lies, as well as with the undeniable historical consequences of our political situation, with the Catalan intellectuals who diagnosed it, and continue to diagnose it, using a variety of arguments. Similarly, the generalised marginalisation of women writers, despite its undeniable reality as history, is most apparent in the words of those who diagnose it and proclaim it, even if this was not their primary aim.

Let me say it once again, without occluding the reality of the traditional oppression of women writers as women in society and within culture, and without forgetting or losing sight of the history of their marginalisation: I feel it is crucial to approach their literary activity on a basis of normality. It is the only way of treating them which will not perpetuate their condition of abnormality, according to the traditional prejudice.

In general terms, this seems an utterly sensible approach. But it also has a practical usefulness, if one considers that nowadays a Catalan woman writer, when it comes to writing, publishing and selling books, faces no more problems than a man – at any rate, none caused by her sex. More than that, women's names often appear in the listings of Catalan best-sellers, prizes are assigned on a non-discriminatory basis and some Catalan women writers have a readership surprisingly bigger than the average (take the example of Carme Riera, whose first book, *Te deix, amor, la mar com a penyora* is a Catalan best-seller). The problems have other sources, for authors with the same starting point.

The area where women are obviously disadvantaged in literature when compared to men is that of the academy. Catalan women writers, and male writers too, can justly complain of the meagre quantity of Catalan feminist criticism and, consequently, of the slight importance given to issues around gender in the critical reception of their work. Maria Mercè Marçal, for example, is one feminist writer who has often observed how much better her work is understood by women readers than by men. Undoubtedly there are very few women, proportionally, with permanent jobs in literary studies. And yet more and more of us are entering this area. The question that has to be put to these women (as to any person interested or involved in the whole area of literature, in any of its aspects) is whether it makes sense to turn sex into a bandwagon, both for reading and analysis (and the same could be said for nationality, nationalism, race, social class and so on). Obviously everyone is free to choose the position he or she wishes to read from. But overdoing things tends to be counterproductive.

The day when a woman (or any person) approaches the work of another woman without feeling they are doing anything extraordinary (and if one could avoid thinking the work was written by a woman and therefore, in a sense, 'special', it would be better still), whatever the topic of discussion, a giant step forward will have been made, probably with very exciting results. If the chosen topic is women's literature, what matters is to study it, talk about it and work on it without always having to repeat the same story of oppression, because that may well make it impossible to visualize other aspects – it may simply re-produce the traditional marginalisation. This is especially the case now that feminist debate (and not only feminist) has brought about changes in practice and in thinking which make it impossible to ignore specific elements and to stick to determined positions, and when this debate is already moving off in different directions.

Nationality, gender, race, sexuality, social class and so on are elements which cannot be erased, as I said earlier, and I want my position in this sense to be absolutely clear. Enough has been said about how literature, like any human activity, is part of the world that produces it, of that world's ideology and politics. But it is above all else an artistic reality and, as such, deserves to be treated as multiple, diverse, multiform and limitless, besides being enmeshed in a determined social and cultural setting. The literature of Catalan women writers, women's literature in general is, above all and primarily, literature. The more adjectives we apply to it, the more we limit it. If we are not careful, we will confine it so much that bit by bit we will destroy it. The justice of the feminist case, like that of all historically oppressed minorities (and there are many) risks tripping itself up each time its renders abnormal, or exceptional, a phenomenon which deserves to be studied freely from a position of absolute respect for the object of study, and from a plurality of angles and perspectives (as many as there are possible texts and readers).

If we allow texts to speak freely to us, trying not to impose any kind of prejudice upon them, conscious that we ourselves are enmeshed ideologically in the society and the history from which we work, they will speak to us just the same about women (and about blacks, children, workers, homosexuals, men and/or Catalans), about sexuality, love, death, life, history, good food and/or innumerable other subjects. And maybe, once and for all, we will prove able to stop propping up the structures we are fighting against. Because if we need an enemy, a centre, an oppressor, or any similar entity, to help us build a different world, a world where diversity and plurality are accepted, maybe that is because at present we lack sufficient faith in the independence, self-sufficiency and value of the project we are engaged in. And if that is the case, this project, in itself, will lack both feasibility and meaning.

Narcís Comadira

Suddenly a Gorgeous Youth Appears, Provoking an Understandable Agitation in Certain Shy and Excessively Analytical Spirits

Like a god rising
new-skinned amidst agitated waters,
you calm the eyes and summon other,
inner storms, within a blood surprised
at keeping a body so different from yours alive,
for yours seems the only body moving upon
the earth. Oh absurd knowledge!
The skin rises, outer boundary, the flesh
which clothes the bones and gives each movement tension,
internal processes, assimilations,
precise secretions,
and are life, subtle soul,
the deep mystery of a gaze.
And then, for consolation, we reflect
that works and action are enough for us.

But the blood, beyond any excuse,
not knowing why, wants beauty.

Epitaph

I ask of you nothing more than a tender glance
over what I was, no shadow of a regret:
think of me changed from a nothing of ash
to a forgotten, timeless panegyric.

The Weather

The whole country is under cloud.
Fog in the northern coombs:
in the mountains, a glimpse
of sunlight at noon.
Rain on the coast. In the heart,
as always, high seas.

Frisson

When you read me (I'm letting my
imagination run away with me now),
you, adolescent
poets of the times to come,
and decipher my words with so much patience, thanks
to your intuition, your illusions and a dictionary,
maybe thinking in very strange patterns,
in a strange and mysterious language
of "s"s and "z"s, weak
enclitic pronouns, hyphens and apostrophes,
like a war message in code
so that a future
enemy won't understand: will you traverse
time heaped up in front of me and
behind you, by then completely lost to us all,
and enter my desolate words,
ruins of a disconnected story,
to find what makes you, what makes me,
me like the old masters, you
like me, neither old nor a master but attentive
to this *frisson*
– let it not be lost! –
traversing like
a shuttle of desire
the oh so stubborn warp of life,
and will you, too, leave fragments in languages
which will be lost, like mine,
so that other adolescents
in other times to come
will decipher your words – all because of a *frisson*! –
and so, from time to time,
from one code to another code,
again and again the same message will wander
– populous herds of words –
until the end of the world,
if the world has an end?

The Cathedral

You climb to it late one afternoon,
leaving the city with its fogs
and the opaque noise of car horns far behind.
There it is in front of you. Without looking at it,
innocent, you make your way into the half darkness.

48

What murmur of lives can be heard,
of suffering and crimes, of blood on fire,
caught in the cracks of the stones?
You, citizen, climbing here to forget,
the cathedral takes you and, imperceptibly,
a curse settles into your bones.

Centuries open to your eyes: the robes
of ancient, drowsy canons
rise from old chests. Processions
of counts and countesses, abandoning
pallid tombs of alabaster.
Interminable fugues emerge
from the organ tubes and from shy smiles.

Don't hide away. Thanks to you, the cathedral
comes alive, awakens: like a cloud
of incense, all the dreams take form,
and the flame of the most distant and ancestral
desires, to which you owe your birth, glimmers.

The city is here, the whole of life
flits between the columns
and the dust of decomposing altars.
So many old doctrines and the shadowy,
subtle terrors of that youthful faith,
the empty words which resonated,
the vigilant, cruel eye of countless twilights,
turned to crumbs by an army of woodworms.

You as well. Can't you see? Look, the stained glass
windows are extinguished slowly, night
approaches and a trembling takes hold of you.
You and the cathedral, like one single flesh,
fear the enchantment enlivening you may shatter.

Abandon this refuge, abandon it,
struggle with clenched fists that men may endure,
and with men, crimes and suffering.
Go down to the city, buy and sell,
get rich and have sons; if you can, conspire.
Pursue in peace the years you have been given,
for nothing will halt the course of life.

You, cathedral, solemn rose, rise
with those who are yours to the more glorious
destiny angels and demons condemn you to:
open and disperse the fragrance of stone.
I want to see how the sun penetrates your sinews,
and crows flutter above the altarpiece
as they await the flesh within the tombs.

November Meditation

Each year, when November comes, and all
the air is so thick with chrysanthemums,
I love to think of all the things that have
passed by already. Time, the maniac,
leads them to us from its antique refuge
so they can support us in the future.

The mournful days return when, infants, we
found ourselves encircled in the dark
hours by nocturnal demons. What a weight
of tears we sullenly hid beneath
the sheets of self-esteem, so the grown-ups
would think we saw no ghosts and were courageous ...

And, later still, the time when the whole world,
it seemed, revolved around an unaccomplished
act, or round a thought. The hours then
were populated with an imprecise
waiting, with languid suffering, with words,
with an obscure and tender trembling.

How much pointless struggling it takes
gradually to give shape to a new man,
how many secret journeys into dark,
impenetrable regions, down the ways
that offer us a ransom from the instincts
races and past years have heaped on us!

Yes, we think, we're young, alive, and everything sings the triumph of strength: a perfect body,
the flame of a desire, the transient smile
in certain eyes, a slender gesture, while
the foreboding that's lain in wait since those
far off beginnings already devours us.

Oh death, oh death, encircling all our steps!
We're born with you, we come to your sweet call
even at the distant start when we are only
a seed seeking a place it can take root.
Woods and seas, birds, different animals,
all await the day of our appearance.

Don't take fright reflecting that the time
you have is counted: the whole world's for you.
You have to energetically dig
your claws into the bit of time that's yours.
Let the pain that fills so many moments
serve to make your muscles' anger harder.

Gentlest November, keep me company,
don't allow me to forget these things.
You move onwards, I know, nothing prevents you
living intensely through each single hour.
I, too, want to escape from unshaped fears,
I've placed a bet on life and I must win.

Southfields 1 edited by Raymond Friel and Richard Price. A new big little magazine. New poetry by John Burnside, Robin Fulton, Elizabeth James, David Kinloch, Edwin Morgan, Tom Paulin, and many others. Essays on Paulin and Muldoon; New Poetries; Scottish Fiction in the 1930s; the art of Joseph Davie; Black Film since the 1960s; What was Wrong with the New Poetry Generation; John Burnside; Kathleen Jamie; Racism and the TUC; and more. Illustrated by Edwin Morgan's photocopioids. £4.00. 180pp. For an extra £1.00 EM's *Colour Supplement* (only available here) will be included. *Southfields 2: Exiles and Emigrés* edited by Raymond Friel, David Kinloch and Richard Price. Living in some other place?... Read this. New poems by James Berry, D. M . Black, Christina Dunhill, Robin Fulton, John Greening, Penelope Shuttle and many more. Fiction by James Cressey and Val Warner. Translations from the Danish of Henrik Nordbrandt and the German of Stella Rotenberg. Victor Serge in the Earthquake Zone (trans John Manson), Peter Manson in Fractal-Land, A Short Film About Ring-Pulls... Alasdair Gray on Walter Scott and John Galt. John Wilson: the Poet that Greenock Shut Up. 184pp. £4.00 *Southfields 3: City and Light* edited by Friel, Kinloch and Price.City-hop on the Southfields Trans-Cyberia Express: Glasgow to Tokyo via London, Lisbon, and Paris. Not forgetting Berlin, Istanbul, Moscow and Karachi (advanced reservation is advised for Paisley, Edinburgh and Stromness). New poems by: Donny O'Rourke, James McGonigal, Gael Turnbull, Joanne Limburg, Robin Fulton, Alan Riach, D. M. Black, Don Paterson, Robin Lindsay Wilson. Translations from the French of Emmanuel Moses, Turkish of Nazim Hikmet, Russian of Gennady Aygi. New prose by Donal McLaughlin, Moira Burgess and Kathleen Jamie. Paul Gordon on the poetry of Edwin Morgan, Jim Ferguson on Robert Tannahill, Bill Broady on Gustav Meyrink, and Robin Purves on Rimbaud and the City of Prose. Art by Gary Anderson and Tracy Mackenna. 166pp. £7.00 (current issue). Forthcoming: new format, *SoFi* 4.1 - Gael Turnbull on St Denys Garneau, A New Sequence by Penelope Shuttle, New Poetry by Peter McCarey, Cahal Dallat, Sheila Hamilton, Paul May, Drew Milne, Derick Thomson, Gary Allen, Desmond Graham, and Gordon Meade. Bill Broady on Dad and the National Health Service, Richard Price on Ian Hamilton Finlay, Peter McCarey on the Canonical Virus, John Manson on Louis Aragon (with translations from his later work). And more...c.64pp. £3. Cheques should be made payable to Southfields Press, 8 Richmond Rd, Staines, TW18 2AB.

Branch Office
Sergi Pàmies

Shut in his office, the branch director is reading the new instructions about transfers and credits for exportation. They have reached him via the usual channel and will apply as from the following month. As he reads, he sets his chair turning and moves his legs rhythmically. Then he puts the folder down on the desk and rubs his eyes energetically. With the tip of his pencil, he draws a spiral on the white page of his diary. He meditates. He'll take his holidays in July and spend the month of August without his family, rediscovering vices and pleasures prohibited by his everyday existence. He smiles as he remembers one summer when he went to a porno show and ended up at home with a red-haired and expert prostitute. He is interrupted by a call from a client wanting to know if shares in the public debt can be declared against tax. They discuss rates and types of interest and agree to return to the question later. After the summer. Getting up to leave, he notices that the alarm light has gone on. He moves swiftly to the door and closes the metal latch. He is afraid. He has never lived through a robbery and doubts whether he can face it with the necessary calm. He goes over the emergency procedures in his head and switches on the electronic locking device for the safe. He turns the key which blocks the opening mechanism. His hands are sweating. He hears a woman's voice shout: "Call an ambulance". He has heard no shot, but maybe the robbers, if they are professionals, have silencers on their weapons. It will be better not to leave the room, he thinks. He will wait until the police arrive. They cannot be long. At security meetings, the management always boasts about the alarm systems, but if the robbers come into his office and find him sitting there, they will kill him when they find he has blocked the safe. There is no point acting the hero. Nervously, he arranges the papers on the desk to give the impression no-one is in the office. Careful to forget no single detail, he decides to hide in the filing cabinet. He moves a shelf, kneels down, gets in and closes the door from inside. He can see the lower part of the office through the fissure. He prays. If they find him, they will try to flee using him as a hostage. The very idea of crossing the avenue with a pistol pressed to his temple, surrounded by police officers and television cameras, makes him tremble. Obviously, he thinks, if he gets out alive, his prestige will increase and maybe they will send him to the main office. The manager calls his name. From the terrified tone of voice it is clear that he has the butt of a gun in his side. A man advises breaking the door down to see if there is someone in the office.

"He must have gone out," says the manager.

Through the fissure, he sees them battering on the door from outside. The police must be here by now. He closes his eyes. Maybe the police are outside, thinking of a way to surprise the attackers with a swift and secure manoeuvre. The woman is still shouting. With a great crash, the door falls in and the manager's legs walk round the room, checking that the director is absent. Other legs, wearing boots, follow on the manager's footsteps. He tries to remember if he has seen those boots before. He is not sure. From now on he will pay especial attention to the most insignificant details of the bank's employees and clients. More legs have entered. Eulalia's, with well-rounded ankles, have paused in front of the cabinet.

"He's seriously injured," she has told the manager, while dialling a three-digit number to call an ambulance.

The boots have disappeared. If someone has been wounded, the robbers must be shaky. But, on the other hand, there is no panic in the employees' attitude. In any case, he thinks, better to stay put. He starts praying again. Now, what he wants is for it all to end, to go home, have a shower and forget the episode. Eulalia goes out. If he were to open the door now, he could talk to the manager and find out what is going on. But he does not lift a finger. He cannot bear the idea that, after this incident, the staff might call him a coward and exaggerate what has happened, merely to humiliate him. If they were to tell central office about his behaviour, he would be subtly punished, condemned to go from one village branch to another, with no further prospect of climbing the career ladder, ruining his own life and his family's in the process. He has difficulty in breathing. The manager talks to some new legs, dressed in white, telling them to take the corpse away, he will wait and speak to the police patrol. The director is getting worried. It looks as if the robbers are no longer there. They must have fled to avoid being charged with robbery and homicide. He starts crying. The legs intertwine; he takes it they are hugging each other. She comments that the family will have to be informed. When you come down to it, she says, that's the director's job.

"He's never around when he's needed," answers the manager.

Judging by the girl's reaction, the dead person could be one of the staff and that will mean real trouble. The union will get involved, wanting to know exactly what happened and who was responsible. He will be named in meetings, assemblies, reports, and probably, instead of promoting him, they will give him the sack there and then, to set an example and win over public opinion and the union. He's sweating so much his shirt sticks to him. He has taken off his tie. He decides to stay there till it is time to stop work. Later he can invent a visit to an important client and, if the dead person is one of the staff, he can express his condolences in first person. After the lunch break, he can order a wreath and pretend the whole business has affected him tremendously.

"I'll call the joiner to replace the door," says the manager.

"Are you coming round tonight?" Eulalia asks him.

The manager is not sure. It depends where all this leads. She leaves the office. Now he realises that if the union carries out an investigation, they will want to know if his version is reliable. It will be hard to find someone to take the risk of giving false testimony. Maybe a bribe would do the trick. His brains are working overtime and he feels more and more trapped. Any decision whatsoever, even the most dignified, looks like a definitive sentence. He mops his forehead and his neck with a handkerchief. The cabinet is an oven, but he has to hold out until it is time to stop work. Three-quarters of an hour to go. He tries to give himself courage by reflecting that anyone else would have done the same in his shoes. What is more, he has saved the bank's money and that is what really counts. The salary they give him does not justify him risking his life confronting criminals who may well be drug addicts. He looks at his watch. More legs come in and somebody announces a police inspector. He closes his eyes. He prefers not to hear what they are saying. The words come through the fissure, pitiless. The manager says the director is away and the incident happened a while ago. The ambulance had to take the corpse off, along with a hysterical woman who was only making things worse. He cannot breathe. The police want to know the tiniest details: the time, exactly where the body fell, how many people were present, etc. He cannot take any more. He wants to leave the cabinet, to confess whatever he has to, in spite of the scorn of his staff, his career, his holidays in July. He makes up his mind without thinking about the consequences and opens the cabinet door violently, just after hearing that a lifelong customer of the bank, an industrialist who dealt in cork, has died. He came into the branch drenched in petrol and set fire to himself, without saying a word. The others do not know the reason, but he knows the man was going through a difficult patch. He remembers how, the week before, he refused to let him have a loan. There were insufficient assets and securities.

Pygmalion in Barcelona

Lluís-Maria Todó

In the second half of May 1997 a Catalan adaptation of George Bernard Shaw's *Pygmalion* was produced in a Barcelona theatre. My readers will be familiar with the play's subject. What I want to do is to examine certain features of the Catalan version. The performers included several of our most celebrated actors, who owe their fame largely to serials and light entertainment programmes on the local channel, TV3. As everybody knows, the point of *Pygmalion* is to dramatise the relations between social classes and their dialects, stressing how crucial it is to use a prestigious speech form if one wants to join society's highest echelons, or at least, to mix with them. I assume this to have been the case in London when the play was written and first performed. But things become more complicated if the intention is not only to translate it into Catalan but to adapt it to a Barcelona setting. Two attempts have been made.

Joan Oliver (1899-1986), a poet and playwright forced into exile after the Civil War, was behind the first Catalan adaptation of *Pygmalion*, performed and published in 1957. He moved the action from Victorian London to present day Barcelona. The low class dialects used by the Catalan equivalents of Eliza Doolittle, her father and her friends, must even then have struck the public as unconvincing. They would also have found the play's main theme – the need to speak Catalan (in this case) if one is to improve one's position in society – far-fetched, given that they lived under Franco's dictatorship. Nevertheless, those dialects persisted in the memory of Joan Oliver and his audience, if nowhere else.

The new version requires a very different interpretation. Taking Oliver's translation as his starting point, Xavier Bru de Sala, a poet and translator born in 1952, introduced substantial changes. To begin with, he moves the action back to 1917, when Barcelona, and Catalonia as a whole, experienced major economic growth (largely thanks to the First World War). There was cultural expansion too, given that Catalonia had acquired its first devolved government in modern times, the Mancomunitat. The upper-class characters in the new version more or less follow the earlier model. But instead of the characteristic dialects of working-class Barcelona, Rosita (Shaw's Eliza) and the other plebeian characters speak a Catalan with strongly Spanish[1] features of vocabulary and pronunciation. Curiously, there is much talk about local Barcelona dialects, and the professor's unfailing ability to identify them, especially in the first act. But we never actually hear them. Why? Because, beyond any doubt, the audience would not recognise them. Working-class areas of Barcelona such as Sants, La Barceloneta or Gràcia retained their own dialects until the 1950s or 60s. Today they have vanished utterly: firstly, due to massive immigra-

---

1. When speaking of the language, Todó consistently writes *castellà*. With some reservations, I translate both this and the word he uses in other contexts, *espanyol,* as 'Spanish'.

tion from other parts of Spain (in particular Andalusia, Murcia and Extremadura); and secondly, to the inevitable standardising influence of local Catalan television, TV3. The result is a striking paradox. The 1997 *Pygmalion* puts Catalan society of 1917 on the stage, whereas in sociolinguistic terms, it is closer to the 1990s than to the years of the Mancomunitat, which were more faithfully reflected in the 1957 version.

All of this is normal enough. After all, we are dealing with a piece of theatre: what matters is that the audience should be able to understand what happens on stage and, most of all, that they should enjoy the performance. And there can be no arguing the fact that, in 1990, a Catalan audience can no longer identify the various dialects that used to be spoken in working class areas of the city. Far from it. They expect people who live there to speak Catalan with a strong Spanish accent, the kind of Catalan known as *xava*.

But I want to move right on to a more perverse (if one can say so) feature of the adaptation: the main theme of the play, the axiom according to which, to climb the social ladder, you have to speak a language 'well', the way rich people speak it. While this may still be the case in London, it has never been true for Catalan in Barcelona. It appears that the privileged classes in Catalonia started speaking Spanish long before the arrival of Franco, and even before the Bourbons ascended the throne, in the 18th century. It is well known that from the 16th century onwards, writers in Catalonia, Valencia and Mallorca abandoned their mother tongue overwhelmingly, in favour of Spanish. No doubt the situation was different where speaking is concerned. Unfortunately, we have no reliable studies of this aspect.

It is simply false to claim that in 1917 anyone needed to speak Catalan 'correctly' to enter fashionable homes or cut a fine figure at an opera ball in the Liceu. Most likely, at those celebrated balls, the upper middle classes and the aristocracy of Barcelona preferred to use Spanish – to be exact, the rather aberrant Spanish they still speak today which was, beyond doubt, the language Joan Maragall, our great national poet, used at home.

Lies of this kind – stage lies, artistic lies in general – need to be understood rather than condemned. Why should a writer offer, and a society accept, such a lie? It strikes me as fair to conclude that it satisfies a half-conscious longing for a dream vision, a different history for our language, the dream of a 'normal' language in a 'normal' country (to use the key word of recent debates), a language just like English, French or Spanish.

It is particularly significant that *Pygmalion*, probably the most metalinguistic play in the classical repertoire, should be staged just now language continues to be the major issue in Catalan society and, since the Partido Popular won the elections in 1996 and made an alliance with Basque and Catalan nationalists, it is a burning cultural and political issue throughout the country. Some facts: the Linguistic Normalisation legislation currently in force in Catalonia takes as its starting point the declaration in the Spanish constitution that Catalan is the *native* language of Catalonia and has the same official status as Spanish. Thanks to what is called 'linguistic immersion', schools in Catalonia use Catalan exclusively as their teaching medium. Any one who wants to work as a civil servant has to prove their competence in the language.

Several months ago, however, the Generalitat (Catalonia's autonomous government) announced its wish to pass further language legislation, to be approved unanimously by all parties in the Catalan parliament. According to them, the new law would consolidate the normalisation of Catalan, considered still to be at risk. Its most controversial provisions are that all products sold in Catalonia must bear Catalan labels, and that the staff of all public institutions and private establishments ('department stores, commercial premises, hotels, restaurants, hospitals, clinics, and all commercial, tourist, health and sports centres active in Catalonia') must deal with clients in the language the latter choose. Failure to comply would naturally bring sanctions. The project has aroused widespread criticism. The socialists, for example, say that you cannot legislate for private conversation between citizens, only for the published word.

Every day articles about language appear in the press, declarations proceed from different groupings, and the representatives of the Partido Popular have refused to be involved in drawing up the law. Particularly important was a declaration by some of Catalonia's most famous Spanish language writers, amongst them Eduardo Mendoza and Felipe de Azúa, that Catalan society today is totally bilingual and that there is no language conflict such as to justify additional legislation. Other groups have claimed the contrary, that Catalan needs further protection and support. The law is currently being revised, but it is extremely unlikely that it will be unanimously approved, as the Generalitat desired.

As if this were not enough, Catalan nationalists in Madrid recently managed to elicit an official pronouncement that the language spoken in Valencia is Catalan. While this is accurate in linguistic terms, and obvious to any educated person, it was seen as an affront by certain people in Valencia, highly irritated by what they consider to be evidence of Catalan imperialist attitudes towards their own specific identity. Quite simply, many people prefer to say they speak Valencian (*valencià*). Relations between the two provinces have never been smooth, and will be even less so now. For some reason, there has never been any trouble with Mallorca, where people speak a dialect they call Mallorcan (*mallorquí*).

Language is the only feasible basis for a Catalan identity, since no Catalan race exists, our cooking is extremely heterogeneous, we dress more or less like people in the rest of Spain and do not have our own religion. It is however impossible to ignore the fact that roughly half of us (and President Pujol himself has defined as Catalan anyone 'who lives and works in Catalonia') have Spanish as mother tongue. Soon there will be others who speak Arab or Swahili. Under these circumstances, some people demand more official protection for a language they believe to be in danger, while others insist that laws are for all citizens, and that you cannot frame them as if nothing had changed, in sociolinguistic terms, over 50 or 100 years.

The cultural policies of the Generalitat of course reflect this situation. Films and plays produced in Catalonia get grants *provided they are in Cat-*

alan. As a result, Catalan cinema, which was never strong, has now vanished completely and definitively, and actors, director and technical staff have had to move to Madrid to find work. The sad reality is that, with few exceptions, no-one wanted to watch the films made in Catalan and financed by the Generalitat. There is a plethora of stage productions in Catalan, but the longest-running play in Barcelona, breaking all the records, is a Spanish version of Neil Simon's *The Odd Couple*, performed every night for more than two years, without a penny of backing from the government.

There are problems and inconsistencies with literature, too. Every year the Ministry of Culture of the Spanish government offers grants to writers and translators in the four official languages of the state: Spanish, Catalan, Gallego and Basque. The Catalan government offers grants as well, but only to writers who use Catalan. This means that Catalan writers and translators who work in Spanish, and whose taxes are used to fund the grants, feel discriminated against. Yet again, those who defend the policy of the Generalitat refer to the years in which Catalan was repressed by Franco's dictatorship, and the need to make up for this by arbitrary measures.

Much the same happens with publishing. Nearly ever book written in Catalan benefits from a government grant known as the *suport genèric*. No-one will deny that this grant has led to a dizzying rise in the number of books published in Catalan. Whether it has led to an improvement in quality is another question. Today more books are published in Catalonia than in most countries with a similar population. Yet nobody would dispute the fact that the great names of Catalan literature belong to the past, often to the Franco years (as with Mercè Rodoreda or Josep Pla), and that today there is no-one of comparable stature on the scene.

As so often happens, the decadence of a literature is linked to the evolution of the language it is written in. Catalan now faces one of the most serious crises in its history, perhaps the most serious of all. I am no linguist, far less an expert in sociolinguistics. Yet I can safely say that what is at issue is a crucial feature of any language people write in, namely, its relationship with living, spoken language. The Catalan that people speak today is alarmingly corrupt. The funny thing is (and the question merits closer study) that this should coincide with the return of independent institutions to Catalonia, the resulting widespread teaching of the language and the setting up of a weighty range of audiovisual communication media in Catalan.

With teaching, a factor which has indubitably influenced the evolution of the language is that, while every schoolteacher must use Catalan in the classroom, many of them do not have it as their mother tongue. They have learnt the language as adults, thanks to the many possibilities for doing so offered to Spanish speakers by the Generalitat. Sadly, these teachers use an artificial, oversimplified form of Catalan, fatally contaminated with Spanish expressions, and this is what their pupils learn (especially the ones who use Spanish at home).

When TV3, the autonomous Catalan channel, started transmissions, a kind of language was needed which would be applicable in new contexts, such as dubbing foreign programmes, in news broadcasts or in live sports events. To begin with, there was heated discussion between those who argued for an archaic, rural style, and those who wanted something more modern and urban. The latter triumphed, or rather, had the lion's part in the compromise which emerged. The resulting style, natural to Barcelona, and which may be considered genuine there, is now spreading, thanks to the prestige of television, especially among younger people, to rural Catalonia, which used to be looked upon as a kind of language 'reserve'.

The difficulty for writers is to devise a medium modern enough not to alienate their readers, while at the same time being sophisticated enough to permit stylistic manipulation. To do so is not always simple. Recently Antoni Puigverd, an outstanding poet, has claimed that Catalan writers are forced to choose between stylistic 'anorexia' (his word) and a rigid, archaic style with ideological (nationalist) and sociolinguistic (rural) overtones they may not all be happy with.

Connected with the foregoing is another problem. Elsewhere, capitals and major conurbations function as a kind of laboratory, where a language can be transformed and rejuvenated. This is not the case with Catalan. Barcelona has nothing to set beside *argot* in Paris, Cockney in London or *cheli* in Madrid, a mode of expression which both deforms and renews the genuine resources of a language. Young people in Barcelona speak a Catalan so contaminated by Spanish, in its lexis, syntax and phonetics, that it is often hard for their elders to recognise it as Catalan. Most people in Barcelona, especially the younger ones, urgently need a set of lessons from Professor Jordana, the Catalan equivalent of Higgins.

So when a novelist or a translator wants to have a young person, someone on the edges of society, or (why not?) a policeman talk, he or she must either abandon verisimilitude, break with the norm, or lose narrative coherence. By the same token, it is unconvincing to have an upper class character in Barcelona speak standard Catalan. If the leading role of Barcelona in contemporary Catalonia has distinct advantages, it may nevertheless have an unforeseeable effect on written Catalan in the 21st century.

Maybe I sound over-pessimistic. Anyone who has visited Catalonia recently must have noticed how many advertisements and public signs are written in Catalan. If a traveller asks, he or she will be told that Catalan has never been so widely written, that more people than ever before can read, write, understand and speak it, and that Catalan television draws the highest audiences in Catalonia. True as this is, I, like many other writers and translators, have to be more wary. However many people answer survey questions in the affirmative, one wonders what they mean by 'Catalan'. Anyone over 40 with a minimally sensitive ear will tell you that under Franco, in the 1950s and 60s, the Catalan used in Barcelona was much more alive, genuine and rich than nowadays.

Since this fact is hard to accept, and even harder to account for, many people take the easy road and demand further laws and grants to 'normalise' our poor language, so maltreated by the Bourbons and by Franco. Every now and then, an intellectual makes some provocative statement, as when Quim Monzó joked, in a recent article, that the life support system should be disconnected, that a sort of linguistic euthanasia should be allowed to take place. Such subtle irony does not go down well with the general public, however, and it terrifies people to hear that Catalan is in danger. That is why the ideological and linguistic manoeuvres of a production like the recent *Pygmalion* should not surprise us. They allow Catalans to imagine, for a couple of hours at least, that their language has been, and above all will be, 'normal'.

Catalan society in the 1990s is more prosperous than ever before and boasts an unprecedented level of social consensus. The two phenomena are intimately connected with one another, and with the successful integration of the incomers who have arrived in Catalonia since the beginning of this century. Maybe the price we have to pay is a kind of de-naturalisation of our language, even its disappearance. That would be a pity. But I cannot help thinking that the history of a language is the history of the people who speak it, laws or no laws.

Illustration by Jane Dunlop

Paula Jennings

Moving Inward, Moving On

Fool

The first card, the O, the circle
full of squirming space,
and through this sacred hoop the young fool leaps
into the young day;
radiant as a crocus,
inches from the cliff's edge,
on each foot, she hopes, a little wing.

Ace of Wands

One-in-fire is will
gathered in a burning bud,
is red for fighting and winning,
throwing off a calyx rough as a cat's tongue,
scarlet silk unfolding like a spring.

Page of Cups

The fish jumped in the cup,
the fish
swam in my left eye;
there were pictures in its scales,
shutters of pearl
opening for me.

Eight of Cups

There is a drumming here,
a grey note.
This is the steepest dream-world.
and I choose to scramble down
through tensions locked at a high whine
to where the light is white cloud cover,
low pressure storm glare, and
losing balance,
I am scattered.
I count my fragments: these are my feet,
these my hands, my head this sobbing camera;
sliding,
I plunge beyond language into my body,
to a grief so whole it feels like joy.

Hanging

On this tree you lose not your life,
but your lies.
They drop from you like rotting fruit
until at last you dangle in the branches,
upside down,
between worlds,
listening to the knowledge of the tree
and smiling like that ancient snake.

Two of Pentacles

Two worlds are tossed in air;
they fly on muscle and movement,
holding their course over and over.
Faster, they are a lemniscate of light,
balanced on nerves and arms and eye.
They are the juggler's certainty
until she wonders
am I artist or deceiver,
and her worlds collide.

The Devil

jumps up and prances,
shakes a leg, shows how it's done:
if you want you can focus on yellow eyes
and feel your fear stretching on and on.
You can keep coming back to that
or you can go on down
past the cold mouth, the sharp arms
with their prongs reaching out to snag you,
the torso like a cliff, and then, shudderingly,
furred haunches with your shame
barely hidden between them,
and you can get stuck here
with grown-up voices burning your cheeks.
You can do all this many times
but if you keep on down
you'll see hooves dancing, drumming
all the rhythms you ever wanted.

Moon

On the moonpath to the sea
old fears flutter out from her in rags,
dark streamers,
but her mouth trumpets lilies
and her feet sing on the wet sand.
She wears her scars like brooches,
cool pearls,
and all her loves, embroidered on her sleeve
in runes and spirals,
glisten in the metal light.
Jester in monochrome,
she splendours this night beach.

Tomatoes

Tomatoes are tricky;
however gently you bite
they spurt their sweet seeds
on your clean shirt.

She sashays down the street;
my eyes are full of the silver
fish on her crimson skirt,
my hands are full of wanting.

I flick an empty line,
I'm a fool with no bait,
but she turns with a rosy grace
and her teeth are gentle.

We bite together,
the seeds are splashing everywhere.

Pentecost

You flap into my dream with a heron's measure
but no cracked cry. You are origami treasure
made from bin-bags, flat black bird
with tiny eyes, ancient and kind.

You know I'm drawn by contradictions,
so you land, graceful litter,
close enough for my hand's shock
as you transform, plastic to pentecostal feathers,
but no meek dove; breast rippling tongues of flame,
wings spanning sacrament as our bellies touch.

Medusa at the Office

I knew it was time to leave
when you saw the snakes in my hair;
I had hidden them with smiles
and perfume to distract you
as I entered the straight lines of your buildings,
the long corridors to my everyday desk.

Through office afternoons
fluorescent blades above me flickered
dissonance until my rhythms turned on me
with teeth. There were edges everywhere
and my face began to scare me, tight and white,
with a stranger's eyes, professional.

Beyond your halted seasons
a voice, sinuous and sweet, would call to me;
my unshed skins stiffening to a cage,
my moons discredited
and every empty dawn your shrill sun
bludgeoning my dreams.

The hissing, when it came, surprised us both,
uncoiling from my rage so fast.
You stared in shock and recognised yourself;
this time I left before the kill.

Festival Hall Without You

Jazz rhythms hurl
waves over these acres
of polished floor, curl
towards me, more than ready to bleed,
womb full, taking up the slack
from my empty heart. The sound hits,
froths around this exhibition of ugliness,
lapping at canvas, acrylic, oils,
failing to bear them off, and I,
failing to bear any of this, adrift
on the shiny wood planks.

This is fitting, I realise, at sea
with these pictures of noisy emptiness.
This is fitting, I tell the gap beside me.

Jim C Wilson

At Edlingham Church, Northumbria, 10th March 1996

At one of Christianity's cradles, mist
is thinning on the moors. Our early walk
is to the castle's broken walls, but first
we pass the church, a low grey place of rock.
And with the singing of the wind, a psalm
blends in with high birds calling. Words of praise
have risen here since Bede, exalting Rome,
grew blind while writing histories. March clouds
prohibit the sun. Chilled, we stand as still
as gravestones. The castle's tower leans, held
only by a new steel strut. Then voices tell
us worship's over. Folk file out; some nod.
A congregation numbering only five,
warmed by calor gas, keeping God alive.

Gifts from the sea

The children seek the shining starfish
and all the gifts the sea should bring.

Their fingers sift in sand as waves edge in
and lock a chill around bare ankles.

The sandcastle softly dissolves,
as plastic soldiers float in the moat,
adrift with a nylon Union Jack.

Then, *Mummy, Mummy, see what I've found!*

As the gulls all shriek, an airforce plane
soars low and shadows the gold of the bay.

*Mummy, quick, hurry and see,
I've found a piece of pirate's treasure!*

A gift that's half a century old
from wise men able to win the world
and burn holes in the palms of children.[1]

---

1. In 1995 thousands of live Second World War incendiary devices were
washed up on the beaches of south-west Scotland. Miraculously, at this
time of writing, only one child has been injured.

Woman of Somalia

"The multinational force of more than 4000 troops has largely been welcomed by Somalis" (Report in the *Scotsman*)

Woman of Somalia, you were a celebrity:
we feasted our eyes on your lovely breasts
which made Page One (in colour)
because a mob of Somali men
stripped and stoned and beat you
because (perhaps although unofficially denied)
a few French soldiers had fucked you.

Woman of Somalia, you were a celebrity
and soldiers watched from the safety of roofs
as you fought for your life
in the heat and the dirt
as the press looked down from the safety of roofs
and their cameras clicked
and let the men of the Western World
fasten our gaze on your naked skin.

Woman of Somalia, you were a celebrity
though your image wraps our rubbish now
with the recipes, sport and fashion.
And the light of fear in your eyes
is gone. Policemen in Mogadishu shot you –
that's justice for a prostitute:

Woman of Somalia, you were a celebrity.
The soldiers and pressmen came down from the roofs
and all the right questions were asked.
A UN spokesman made a pronouncement
and the troops drove into the desert.

Woman of Somalia, you are timeless
and you have no name. As the men closed in
you grabbed for a knife; it flashed in the sun
then fell to the earth. I will remember you
shining, in your millions, like the stars.

Troywood

The bunker's sunk beneath a field; ten feet
of concrete keeps it safe from flash and blast
and fall-out. Leaders would escape the heat
while we stacked sandbags, melted, breathed our last.
Deep down in the earth there are lines of bunks
awaiting personnel. There's pristine air
for the chosen few, who'd retreat like monks

66

to contemplate screens, be witness to despair.
Entombed in the ground is a chapel. Cold
War deaths are recalled in brass, on a plaque
devoid of names. A tape played as we strolled
among the vacant pews, and felt the lack
of sanctity. An absent congregation
sang battle hymns for our world's cremation.[1]

Away from it all

In hot bastides, and on Grecian shores,
the young of Europe are on vacation.
They're chauffeured in Volvos and BMWs;
they have magazine teeth, designer hair.

They're bored as they pick at soft cloth napkins
while their parents expand through the evening.
I watch from the street, from across the tables;
I'm a million trillion light years away.

Their glazed eyes say, *Must we tolerate this?*
While their pouts shape up for something better.
And I cry as though from a tower of grey stone,
I used to go to Burntisland!

My thin lips purse as I sip cheap wine
and feel the east wind start to blow.
It pulls at the thinness of my shirt;
its fingers are tickling my protestant heart.[2]

Soul Triolet

By Twinlaw Cairns on Lammermuir
my soul fills up with emptiness.
Curlews' calls are white like the moon,
by Twinlaw Cairns on Lammermuir.
The winds have stroked the landscape smooth;
the skies come scouring from the west.
By Twinlaw Cairns on Lammermuir
my soul exults in emptiness.

1. In 1952 a secret underground command centre was constructed at
Troywood in East Fife. In the event of a nuclear attack, the Secretary of
State, military commanders, and staff were to go there, and seal themselves inside. The bunker is now open to the public
2. Burntisland exists on the north coast of the Firth of Forth. It has an
aluminium works and small run-down docks. It used to have a very
cold open-air swimming pool.

Illustration by David Schofield

It Takes One to Know One
Leslie Schenk

A general practitioner's consultancy, much like GP consultancies the world over. One conspicuous difference. The drab neutrality of the colours of the wallpaper (beige), hand-me-down furniture (natural varnished wood) and rug (greige) are set off by brilliant, framed-under-glass posters for art exhibits, mostly Continental, a Delacroix, a Morandi, a Van Gogh, several Monets, all of different dimensions but skilfully juxtaposed, so that scarcely any vomitous beige is noticed, usually.

Dr Scrimshaw has evidently given some thought to the inexpensive decoration of his consultancy. Reproductions of paintings look cheap, he has surmised, whereas reproductions of posters featuring those same paintings look chic, if there can be such a thing as chic in this semiposh outer suburb, Hinsdale, and if the occasional French wordings across them smack of pretentiousness, *tant pis!*

Seated before him at his desk, Dr Scrimshaw's patient seems impatient to unburden herself of a well-rehearsed list of complaints, but not too impatient to take in the posters behind his head, especially a Monet snow scene.

She is ancient, his patient, nearer to eighty than to seventy, extravagantly well-groomed although without any jewellery visible, the fabric textures of her clothing expensive and 'colour co-ordinated' as the adverts say, and yet she wears no make-up, which seems odd in the setting of the rest, despite her age. Well, Dr Scrimshaw tells himself, you could have fooled me. For he has just noticed that her natural-looking blond hair, drawn back, culminating in a bun, is grey and white at a uniform distance from her forehead: surely a significant symptom.

"You're different," the woman tells him.

"Of course," Dr Scrimshaw answers. "Aren't you?"

"Too different." Her face clouds. "That's the trouble."

"Your name, please." This GP has to fill in his cards himself, for he cannot afford a receptionist.

"Marguerite Harrower."

"Address? Phone number?"

She provides them, and Dr Scrimshaw carefully jots them down. He looks up, thinks, She is examining my features as assiduously as I am examining hers. What can be her trouble? She looks all right. Still has all her marbles, I should say. Constipation, sleeplessness, or both, I should guess, caused by anxiety, deep terrible destructive anxiety. How well I know that state: – how often have I felt *I* should be a patient but there's no one to play doctor to *me*.

What a nice looking young man! He will understand. He is not like the others, no, not at all. There is that something in his look that portends a mind opened to possibilities beyond the Hinsdale humdrum. And how nice, that smile before he speaks –

"And what can I do for you, Mrs Harrower?"

"Miss."

"Ah. Miz Harrower."

"Not Miz. *Miss* Harrower."

Scrimshaw swivels in his chair while formulating his thought. "I am not one to conclude any dire significance from that, I can assure you."

"You do reassure me, doctor. I knew you were different."

"We're all different, wouldn't you say?"

"No, I wouldn't. Most of us are peas in a pod."

"Well, I know what you mean, but ... "

"But?"

"But it doesn't get any of us very far, running around saying so." Scrimshaw pulls himself together and takes on his set professional air, deepening the vertical line between his brows so that he should look more than forty, arching the tips of his fingers of both hands aloft to form the shape of a cathedral. It is particularly difficult, he recites to himself, to take on an efficacious aura of infallibility before someone twice your age.

"That's a miraculous painting in the poster above your head."

Scrimshaw has to swivel around to identify it, then looks pleased at the comment.

"Even the blue shadows in the snow banks contain light, don't they?"

"Just like our minds, Miss Harrower, when we are severely depressed."

"Yes. Except not always."

Scrimshaw is at once appreciative and surprised that his ambiguous simile is so instantly understood. Despite their age difference then, he reckons he will not, after all, have to take on the undeserved accoutrements of wisdom, authority and expertise doctors usually feel essential to assume, in the probably well-founded belief that such masks add half the potency to their prescribed medication, usually embellished and reinforced by diplomas on walls and stacks of well-bound volumes – volumes never referred to in the presence of patients. Scrimshaw feels relaxed now, almost jovial, although the problem of Miss Harrower's ailments, if any, remains.

"But you really must tell me why you have come to see me."

Silence. How can I tell him, in a way that will get through to him?

"Is it that you are new to Hinsdale?"

"Oh no, I've lived here since before this place became attached to the City and got itself swallowed up by contiguous suburbs. No, it's not that."

"Well then, don't you have a GP you consult regularly?"

"Oh him. I've given up on him years ago. He thinks double-talk and placebos will cure anything, and I suppose with most people they do." A pause for a comment from Scrimshaw, which is not forthcoming. "Also, I rarely have anything wrong with me, physically, especially since I've been getting 'flu shots every year. I'm stronger than young people in all aspects but one. You're the third new doctor I've seen in as many weeks."

"So that now, psychologically ... "

"Exactly."

"Which makes it infinitely more difficult to talk about, doesn't it?"

"I knew you were different. I knew you would understand."

"I can understand nothing until I drag something more descriptive out of you." Scrimshaw attempts to sound gently humorous, and succeeds.

"The thing is ... The thing is ... Ah, 'difficult' is not the word for it. 'Excruciating', rather; 'devastating'. I don't know; 'killing'."

"I know."

"Do you?" With anxious eyes, Harrower re-examines Scrimshaw's face, or rather the being behind that face, and is reassured again. "Yes, I can believe you do." She draws herself up and plunges in with new courage. "The thing is ... The thing is ... "

"Yes?"

"Well, the thing is threefold. First, I cannot fall asleep. I simply cannot. The blood races through my veins and I can *hear* it, and, depending on how I put my pillow around my ears, it becomes a drumbeat, a *savage* drumbeat. It's awful. And second, I eventually do fall asleep, generally toward five in the morning, and then I have the most extraordinary nightmares. They inevitably culminate in my screaming aloud so that I wake myself up. When I awaken I can still hear my scream reverberating in my bedroom. And I think how fantastically clever I am to have invented the scenario of my nightmare. For a few moments I can recall the plots, and they are intricate reconstructions of things in my life, working themselves out, or perhaps *not* working themselves out, since ever-new versions of them come onto the screen every night. I mean they are absolutely absurd and yet, in their way, works of art. Yes, works of art. I am not a creative person, doctor, yet asleep I become a small-scale Shakespeare or Wagner, or more appropriately really, a Goethe, every night a Walpurgis Night."

Against all his principles, Scrimshaw blurts out, "I have known comparable periods of suffering in my lifetime."

"You have? Am I not alone then?"

Scrimshaw gives a fake cough, and becomes *Doctor* Scrimshaw again.

"Normally, doctors prescribe soporifics and tranquillisers at such times."

"That's what they all offer me. But artificial inducement to sleep has nothing to do with what's ailing me."

"I know, because they never do, and I'm glad you know. But please continue. The third aspect?"

"Ah, that is the most awesome to come out with. You will be the first person on earth I shall have admitted this to."

Her face is so contorted with pain and anguish that Scrimshaw doesn't dare utter another word of encouragement. He just waits, waits longer than he can bear, nearly. I am identifying with this woman, which I know I must not do. I risk becoming as disturbed as she is. But I ask myself, Isn't silence now the best form of understanding? and I reply, Yes, it is.

"You see, if it were just a matter of forgetting things like names or when I walk purposefully into the kitchen with a certain object in my hand and I can't for the life of me remember why, I would know it was simply the onset of Alzheimer's disease."

"No, you wouldn't. It's perfectly normal for elderly people to become so preoccupied with one thing or another of permanent importance to them that they momentarily forget current concerns. Sometimes they're busy inventing dialogue, thinking up what they should have said in the first place, during some difficulty twenty, thirty years back. So much accumulating as the years go by that the past comes to preponderate over recent ephemera."

"Oh. I understand. That doesn't sound so much like medicine as it does like a personal philosophy, but it's good, very good, even. It helps. However, I still await the morning I shall put bread in the coffee machine and pour water into the toaster!" After the cackle of her laugh, the look of anxiety returns like the proverbial cloud obliterating the sun. "Only there are other phenomena, phenomena that constitute stress, deep down-to-earth stress. I can take anything but stress. It exhausts me. It befuddles me."

Scrimshaw's cathedral of fingers become fists. "No more so, surely, than stress befuddles everybody." He looks toward his window, his only visible outlet onto the world. "And yet stress is only a word. The thing itself is so much more than its word. But then that's like everything else."

"The nail on the head!" Harrower declares. A deep sigh scarcely has time to follow and the previously circumvented truth comes pouring out in a rush, hindered no longer.

"Lately, present company excepted, everybody I encounter, everybody, seems to me insane. Well, surely when everybody on the outside seems insane to me, I must be the one to be insane on the inside, no?"

She takes Scrimshaw's apparently impassive attention for a cue to continue, to elaborate, to plunge deeper.

"It started around a month ago. I went into the City to see an opera. I like opera. Maybe that's why my nightmares are so clever, so full of *Sturm und Drang*. I can still weep at a suicide in Nagasaki even though I know perfectly well no one sings at moments like that, the singer is not even Japanese and paper cherry-blossoms don't turn this all-too-drab kingdom into colourful Japan, but there you are, art works for me. I suppose I'm the only person in Hinsdale to like it, opera."

"No, you're not."

A complete change of tone, indignation now. "Then why was our one classical music FM station converted to this dreadful cacophony that rutting secondary-school students consider music?"

Scrimshaw's stern attentiveness turns momentarily into a bemused benevolence. "Isn't that a separate subject we could better discuss some other time?" he suggests, sweetly.

"Perhaps. Anyway, I had no inkling anything basic might be wrong with me until, while poor Cho-Cho-san was catching her breath during the interval, I saw a woman promenading through the foyer with, I suppose, her husband. She was dressed to the teeth, as was I, mink stole, diamonds, the works, face massaged and creamed and made-up all peaches and rubies as was mine, which takes – which took – some doing. And she was chewing gum! Chomp, chomp, chomp! I couldn't believe my eyes. She must be insane, I thought. But nobody else seemed to notice, let alone care. That was the first time it occurred to me I was going, well, bananas, gaga."

Scrimshaw gives a noncommittal grimace and shrug of the shoulders to indicate as unobtrusively as he can that, so far, no big deal.

"That night, back home, I gaped at myself in the bathroom mirror. I stared and examined myself in a kind of horror. My drooping crepy skin was embalmed in thick goo, my lips were outlined in a shade of scarlet no women but prostitutes would have worn when I was a girl, my eyes were outlined in black like an Egyptian mummy's, the shadows under my plucked and pencilled brows were lightened in two shades of luminous blue, the colour of my hair was not real, as you can still see, and at the time it was held together by spray in a bouffant wave ... I couldn't believe it. What on earth could have transformed the real me into *that?* I wondered. And I have come up with no answers."

"Unless," Scrimshaw ventures, "the incessant bombardment of advertising ... ?"

"Well, yes, of course, but something other, more personal than that, too, don't you think? You're right though because, the very next time this agonising certitude about my going insane came over me, I was watching an ad on TV. Oh, it wasn't even the first time I saw this ad or thousands like it, but somehow now, this time, it burnt holes in my brains, so to speak. The gist was that one certain detergent washed 'whiter' than all other detergents on earth. I listened to the syrupy voice of the announcer, the jubilant exclamations of the happy housewives who had somehow discovered this extraordinary product, in reality surely indistinguishable from all other such products, and I summoned up in my mind the march of technical progress that had no doubt started in Neanderthal caves across the Channel, the efforts we have expended before and after 1066 to bring us through floods, fires and wars, the Marne, Coventry and Dunkirk, to bring us through to this, just this, this ridiculous ad, and breaking into the middle of an old stupid but divine Joan Crawford saga at that, and I said to myself, 'No, this is not possible. This is insane. The Magna Carta and the Armistice at Compiègne were not signed for this to happen.' Yet everybody else accepts this kettle of fish. So it must be I who am insane, right? What other alternative is there? I see none."

An awkward silence, but Scrimshaw is more determined than ever to use silence as the token expression and embodiment of sincere sympathy.

"Your just listening to me already helps, I think. But there's worse, and this worse has convinced me that yes, I am going insane; stark raving crackers." To gain a breathing space, Harrower permits her eyes to wander to the posters to her right. They alight on a Renoir outdoor scene of people wading through deep grass punctuated by poppies, on their way to a picnic perhaps, with unseen trees overhead, she supposes, since coins of sunlight can scatter over the scene the way they do only through clumps of leaves, barely suggested in the portion of the painting reproduced in the poster. If dabs of colour on a canvas can become realer than any reality, she thinks, there must be a connection between art and insanity. "I think I've seen that painting before, in Paris or London or someplace."

"You're lucky."

"What money can do isn't luck."

"No, nor is what the psyche can inflict upon its owner."

Harrower emits a very sane laugh. "If you don't mind, I think I could better ponder that, too, some other time, as you more or less said a moment ago." The scowl of inner pain returns as though uninterrupted. "No, but this isn't funny. To know, absolutely *know,* that you're going insane is ... indescribably horrible! Horrible! And it happens in such a workaday way. I pick up a newspaper, turn on the news, and it happens, this overwhelming conviction that what my eyes perceive cannot be the truth, must be hallucinatory on my part, a waking nightmare. And if so, how can I ever trust my judgement on anything, on when to cross a street, for example? In my most potent nightmares I should never be able to invent the concatenations of world events seemingly fabricating themselves before my eyes as I gaze, the corruption and the killing and the really suicidal arrangements made by respected world leaders, and at such times I look out my windows to see if anyone else watching the same telly news I have been staring at aghast is not running out into the streets screaming, screaming, screaming, but no, there is never anyone, and I can hardly hold myself back because I want, need desperately, to run out into the streets myself and draw people's attention to what is happening (usually women and children bleeding because of what some men have perpetrated), and I know this is madness, utterly ridiculous pointless madness, because if I am the only one on earth to see these things it can only be because I am mad, bonkers, nuts, berserk, deserving to be locked up, tied down, strait-jacketed or put to death through some beneficent injection, and strewth!, I think I'm going to cry now, and I never do that, haven't done that in decades!"

And the tears do flow, but not in torrents, only one glistening bead from each eye. Both cease trickling an inch or two further down a well-scrubbed cheek.

Scrimshaw vaults up from his swivel chair and escapes to the window, where, with his hands clenched behind his back, he no longer has to look at his patient, or, what it feels like, look into her soul. He knows his own juices, not tears, the wrong juices, gastric juices, are flowing now. And what am I supposed to say to this woman, he asks himself. Or rather, how am I to say it? What words can possibly convey ... ? He is at complete loss. No, there are myriads of people down there in the High Street, he sees outside his window, scurrying about below, buying lawnmowers or detergent, but no one, not one, showing any concern for or even the vaguest awareness of the slaughter that is going on, not only overseas but right here in the suburb of Hinsdale and even more so in the City it depends on, not one, and even if there were one, what good would it do? And how explain it? 'All we can do is live our lives?' 'Get on with it?' 'Donate money to the Red Cross once a year?' 'Zap the news and look at movies instead, showing how the shooting off of guns is the proof of true masculinity?' And so on, on and on. Do I dare tell Miss Harrower any of this? How could I even put a fraction of it into words, that it is not she but the world that is ... whatever the world is? Words are so poor, so inadequate. She needs something beyond words, but do I have what it takes to give her that other something? And who am I to preach anything whatever at her, at anyone else? Am I any better off than she is? She is no more bananas than I am, or rather I am just as bananas as she is, the same thing. Now I have to speak, I know I *will* speak, and yet I have no idea what I have to say.

Scrimshaw resumes his seat before his patient as casually as he can, locks his eyes into hers again, and feels his mental muscles groping, groping not for an impressive placebo but for something that will work with genuine potency.

"Can you help me, doctor?" Harrower pleads, her eyebrows, newly growing in, forming a faint inverted V.

Scrimshaw plunges in. He unprecendetedly takes both his patient's hands into both of his, squeezes them gently, and looks at her with as warm and omnipotent a sense of affinity as it is possible for him to take on at will. It is usually futile, I know, to attempt to send messages without words, but sometimes it works, and I will it to work now. And I can only hope it will be enough.

"We're all right," he says, hoarsely.

"'We'?"

"Why yes. I understand you, right down to the core of the earth we stand upon, and now you must understand me and believe me when I affirm and reaffirm: we're all right. You see, it takes one to know one, as they say."

"What? What does that *mean?*" Harrower is startled, obviously, and the reason, too, is obvious to Scrimshaw. It is because something profound is finally stirring within her, previously immobile, a moment ago petrified, now liquefying. Knowledge that has always been present, hitherto secret, seeps into her conscious recognition the same way that, through osmosis, a plant absorbs moisture, which, once in, cannot get out again till it rises to the top and either contributes to "growth" or evaporates.

Harrower "grows". For this new comprehension floods over her as though from a submarine volcano, resembling, in the light it gives off, a species of unvoiced decipherment, the kind of non-verbal but self-evident significance and finality of a tab of litmus paper changing colour, but that yet cries out for verbalising, on the false grounds that only verbalisation engenders reality: pink means acidity, blue means alkalinity. Her lips haltingly attempt to form words again. "Could you possibly mean … ?"

"Yes."

"You astonish me. You really do. I thought … well, now I don't know what I thought. Or what to think." Except that, she thinks, I should have been able to figure this out without your telling me. In fact I *have* figured this out without your telling me. For you haven't told me. You have actually *said* nothing. Or else everything, but in silence, which seems impossible, and yet …

The pause extends itself for one of those interminable moments customarily labelled as "pregnant", while Miss Harrower apparently puts her pieces together in a new way. Then, not unlike returning to life, or at least not unlike re-entering a role she has just had confirmed to her she absolutely has to continue to play, ever so artfully, for the rest of her days, she picks up her purse and speaks, in a tone as new as it is old.

"How much do I owe you, doctor? Ah, I know how much I owe you, but what is your fee?"

In his audible reaction to that, a kind of genteel guffaw that he knows surprises them both as he utters it, Scrimshaw fathoms in his deepest depths that he has succeeded in skilfully navigating his very own self, too, back to port, back to safety, back to his customary disguise of what is facetiously called 'normal' stability, however makeshift his version of all that may or may not someday prove to be.

"You want to pay me a fee?" he light-heartedly teases Miss Harrower. "Now *that* would *really* be insane!"

And they both burst into laughter, grim laughter, but laughter all the same, the shared laughter of necessary acquiescence to, if not full acceptance of, the facts.

Scottish Literature E-mail Discussion Groups

STELLA, the centre for development of software and computing facilities and services in Glasgow University connected to the Dept. of Scottish and English Literature and Language, has set up an e-mail discussion list for Scottish Literature. Such a list, which you can join if you have e-mail access, can serve as a shared 'notice board' for discussions and queries.

There are three different lists; literature up to 1700, literature of the 18th century and literature of the 19-20th centuries. You can subscribe to all three at once. We hope that you will join one or all of these lists and then use them, either passively by just reading the messages from other subscribers, or more actively by sending messages and reactions to the list. In this way the list can bring together otherwise isolated readers, scholars and enthusiasts. It should function as a kind of running newsletter for anyone interested in Scottish literature of any period as well as a continuing forum for discussions on a rapidly expanding subject.

If you would like to join the list we can send you a simple one-page information sheet explaining how you can join the list (at no cost) and what the list can do for you. To get this sheet, contact Jean Anderson at STELLA, 6 University Gardens, Glasgow G12 8QH, e-mail: jganders@arts.ac.uk.

Andrew McNeil

A Warm Welcome

Nancy, France 1982

He lay there deein.
A late diagnosis o meningitis.
Doctors no popular
Wi ma French pen-pal:
Catherine still smilin;
Phillipe aw six fit plus,
Haun raised in greetin;
His strength o spirit leavin
A grip on me fresh
As the image o his body sae still.

Her mither huid nae English
Servin me muckle bowls o coffee,
Sae polite tae her visitor fae Ecosse.
Gied ma washt claes a smell
They've niver huid since:
Thair warm welcome niver forgotten,
A journey aye repeated ony time
Ma nose picks up the smell
O fresh baked breid an guid coffee.

Timekeepin

"Ye telt us fower o'clock."
"The bus would arrive at three-thirty at the latest."
"I ken but the letter said somethin aboot fower ... "
"We've had them back for twenty minutes."

Granfaither an teacher:
The ane, fingers still rock-calloused,
Lang since idle fae wark in a Fife mine;
Th'ither, fantoosh as his Apple Mac
Whaur yon note fer thair trip wis ran aff,
Reflections o cooncil hooses
Temporary fer near fifty year noo
No seen throu his windae.

The hill ahint the schule luiks like the Bastille –
Heavy, earthen-haunched,
Barefit ledges oot fae gorse-skirts –
An open-moothed winter stare.

He leaves thankin the heidmaister,
Five bairns o various heichts skirl aroon,
Cries held fer a second
In the late November air.

The May

The blue his a spirit o its ain
Lappin aff the white cliffs
Seen fae Ainster lik cloods.

Awthin is paced oot fer human feet
Frae larach tae cliff tae the beach;
Fowk sharin the island wi rock an gull.

Gien sum maumie winds
A sun makin gannets hyter on ledges
Thon group maun be takin a hairst
A hairst sae deep rootit in the first element.

Yon chiels ur the diggers fer banes
No the monks an invaders o yestreen.

Thai mibbe dinna ken the saut
The yammerin fae shore an sky steys

Steys, steys an rests:

Eneuch tae defeat granite
Thrumple marble
Seep throu steel.

Hame

Every twa year cum hame:
As lang as she cuin dae this
Thai'll be happy in the States.

Pop ower fae America
Whar awthin is bigger
Aye! Standart o life is better.

Stuidin thare it blinds me
What kin of life?
Whase standarts?

She'll no see the young grou
Deid – claes in her mine will cover
The thoosand weys thai an aw us
Gang forrit:
Personal, local an national daeins soak us
Mony ettlin fer better days aheid
Especially noo.

Yon redd squirrel I seen speed across the Muchty road,
A nip o fragile broon beauty framed
Bi the Lomonds – twin baps in ever changin licht
Thai ur lost tae her.

The faimily walk doun the High Street
Ignorin the exhibition poster:
Fae Agricola tae Châtelard unner Queen Mary's bed
Sex an deith hae starrin roles in braw waa panels.

Danderin on-fitsteps echo
Unseen up a close, souns like spirits tappin
No shair o the wey.

Sheena Blackhall

Sonnet for Nuala Ni Dhomhnaill

Each listener was a moth to her light drawn
Her Irish brogue went lilting like a song
Each image floated, lovely as a swan
Trailing its thought-wave-ripple all along
The reading room, where like a new-ploughed field
The loam of every mind lay opened wide
A golden acreage was her poems' yield
Ni Dhomhnaill, potent as a corn bride.

A laugh as deep's the Shannon at her throat
Her heavy pleat hung down, a Celtic braid
Russet with copper, amber overlaid
With bronze it shone as sleek's a fox's coat
And like a torc, her wit and wisdom turned
Brilliant and bright. And like a flame, they burned.

Waitress, Rose Street, Embro

Twa o the smaa oors' clock.
Hard's an angeret skelp, the neon licht's
An oolet, blinkin een tae glisk the nicht.

She shakks crumbs doon. A hummle, hodden, moose
Her een, beady an broon,
Frae caunlelowe, cigar an nicotine, smert wi the rikk.
She takks fowks' orders, prikked bi orra spikk
O customers fa sikk a hantle mair
Than maet an wine, ooto the cauldrife air.

Sma-boukit, fite-faced vratch
She glides amang the claikin cliques o diners
Hashed on aa sides, she battens doon the hatch
A service tug, 'tween transatlantic liners.

Her pooch is threidbare. Foonert on her feet
She serves the late-nicht custom frae the street.
A single mither, skivvyin an skint
Ae powk awa, frae Puirtith an Wint.

The Powser

The powser's sleepin like a clootie dall
At ilkie neuk his cleuks hing doon, twa fauld
His sprauchled kyte's a drift o snawy fur
His thrapple ripples wi a rochlin purr.

His breist-bane swalls wi pech, a bellows blawin
Like a wee boatie, bobbin up, syne faain
On the great sea o sleep, the landlocked powser
Shoogles ae lug, an runkles up his mowser.
An sic a mowser! It micht string a fiddle,
A sailor's riggin, or a fairmer's riddle!

This spurgie's Bogieman, his wame stap-fu
Sleeps douce an gentle as a cushie-doo
Bit aince ootower the yett, the doo's a Deil
A sleekit shadda wi a hairt o steel!

Slidderin alang the glaury, gloomy toun,
His een, twa slits o green, gley up an doon.
The muckle, sherp-pronged trap that is his mou
Gants reid an glimmrin. Cheepers, saft as oo
Chitter an squeak ... the makkins o a meal
Tasty as herrin in a fisher's creel.
Their wicker nest's a puir defence gin Daith
Sud powser chuse tae snip the threids o Braith.

He'll skreich an spit. A rowth o battle scars
Tell o his tulzies, in aneth the stars
King o the cassies' gaun-aboot-nicht-fowk
The powser reigns supreme. He's nae man's gowk.

Tattie Howkers

Spirkit wi sleet, the howkers wirk the rigs
A raw o dreepin nebs booed ower the yird.
Humfin the skulls, hauns dirlin wi the cauld
Liftin the tattie crap wi feint a wird.

Like human brigs, twa-fauld, they stride the glaur
Dellin the dubs fur tatties, clorty-neived
Weet mochles, pirled wi styew, they plyter on
Till ilkie pikk o park is howked an seived.

A line o choochin ingins, puffin rikk,
The braith o bairnies, rises frae the dreel.
At fly-time, halflins ett their pieces thick –
In this, a different drudgery frae the skweel.

Back-brakkin darg. Loons warm tae the wark
Their elders tcyauve ahin, coats auld, an torn
Brikks stapped in waldies. Tattiebogle duds.
Driven bi thocht o cash in haun, the morn.

Ode to an Unkind Reviewer

I did not relish your review.
It took a hanging judge's view,
Of what my Muse attempts to do.
Now, had I been a Saxon toff,
I might have laughed ... have shrugged it off,
As would an academic Don,
With tea leaves for testosterone ...
But you, my dear, lampooned *a Celt*
A creature with a prickly pelt.
My race keeps grudges to the grave.
When we are kicked, we do not cave,
And whimper like a pricked balloon ...
We weigh your venom, spoon for spoon.

I pray your dentist takes the shakes,
E-coli crown your cornflakes.
May your physog be pox-embossed,
Your fax be lax. Your wires be crossed,
Your body odour on the air,
Be ripe's an Arab's underwear.

May your amour be impotent's,
A blob of jellyfish that's spent.
May his libido never rise,
And cellulite engird your thighs.
And when you slide beneath the covers,
May plaque and dandruff grace your lovers.

I call on all the gods of wrath,
To set a tide-mark round your bath.
Your rancid writings, turn to ash,
Your crass computer, screech and crash,
Your friends be few. Your days be numbered,
Insurance contract be encumbered
With horrid clause in tiny print ...
Your house burn down, and leave you skint.

Long may your morning coffee curdle,
Your winners fall at every hurdle,
The fusty fruit of your sad loins,
Be worthless as devalued coins.
Your mats have mildew. Greasy stains,
Lurk in your pipes, and block your drains.

Should you possess a motor car,
May it break down outside Stranraer,
With balding brakes, and leaking oil,
And tank, like kettle on the boil.

If fashionable shoes you buy,
I hope they slip and make you fly
Face foremost, in a mound of dung ...
Flat pancake into treacle flung

May all your canine chums have rabies,
Your cat have fleas. Your gerbil, scabies.
Your table catch Dutch elm disease.
A cloud of locusts eat your peas.
Your hair turn green. Your molars rot,
Your fillings rust. Your scribblings, blot.
Your windows leak. Your bedposts crumble,
The chimneys from your rooftop, tumble.
May death watch beetles chew your plugs,
Your linen cupboard jump with bugs.
Your TV, cooker, fridge break down,
Just when the engineer's left town.

When your dry dust to earth is laid,
May it with DDT be sprayed,
Miss Vampire, spewing froth and spite,
Who feeds upon what others write.

So sour and vinegary you are,
You'd make a champion pickle jar,
More tart than acid drop, by far.
Before you wield your bitter pen,
Your inky guillotine again,
Draw in your claws, and count to ten ...
For should you others, drub, alas
This Celtic curse, may come to pass.

A Story by Borges

Simon King-Spooner

I

Perhaps it was a misunderstanding: one of the improbable and fertile kind that so characterised the time. Perhaps, indeed, the whole era was a misunderstanding, immeasurably tiresome in its scale and complexity.

London, it was; a summer in the late sixties. The petulant snarl of the traffic and the trapped, oven-like heat a single suffocating mass; and at the edge, as if mockingly, certain novel and insidious odours: patchouli, cannabis, joss sticks, sex.

And yes I still see Ginnie, in muslin and Greek sandals, throwing bread to the ducks in Finsbury Park, the stylish abandon of the gesture a little marred by self-consciousness. And I recall that as we walked back, idly observing the slow synchrony of our steps, she told me of a story by Borges.

Or did she? For I have never since pinned it down; though lately, in another capital, another age, I have trawled the catalogue of the National Library assiduously enough, imagining the tale to be a kind of key to that summer – at one with its undertow of sinister absurdity, a fellow to the facetious nightmares that unfolded in the Oz strip cartoons, and behind the eyelids of every sprawled dope-smoker in every mauve-walled bedsit.

Could she have lied? Or did I dream the whole thing? Maybe she meant another author – Calvino? Marquez? Had they been heard of? Then again, maybe the story has never been translated: she read Spanish well – does my mind's eye see 'Borges' on the cover of one of the dog-eared paperbacks in that commendable tongue, inherited from a previous lover, that drooped cobwebs in a corner of her brick-and-floorboard shelving?

Howsoever. If I am to read a story whose outline I have known for twenty-five years, that the sentimental curiosity of my middle age ever more insistently demands, that I have always assumed I would someday find and read, what else for it?

I must write it myself.

(Plagiarism within plagiarism: the appropriation not only of a story and a style, but of the idea of that appropriation – I speak of Borges' Pierre Menard, who endeavoured to regain Cervantes' world, and rewrite Don Quixote. But as Borges, anyway, declared himself a pasticheur of Borges, where in this hall of mirrors did plagiarism begin?

But enough.)

II

Machado Ignatiez – whose name, like all names, was a multitude of references, a beachhead on the unthinkable terrain of the newborn, a hopeful invocation, a prison – leaned heavily on the low sill of the open window, an empty wine glass in his hand. He watched absently as a woman in the street below sprinkled the pavement with water and swept it with a long-handled broom. She was invested in the exorbitantly mundane garb of the lowest class, and sang disconnected snatches of a song of gauchos and of tragic love; her voice, in which the fierce gutturals of Andalusia echoed faintly, was younger than her face, which was younger than her figure. It was that subtle and pensive time between afternoon and evening when – if the recollection of a line of the incomparable Fourth Eclogue may be permitted – the day sighs gently, and eases a little in its harness. The air was growing cool.

Shifting from his reverie, Ignatiez drew himself upright. The room behind was spacious, yet revealed a discerning austerity in its contents: a bed, with Irish linen; a wicker chair on which the latest work of a fashionable Colombian novelist lay open, spine upwards; a wardrobe and a chest of drawers, the otherwise innocent surface of the latter troubled by a small mirror. It was to the chest that he turned, the wine glass still in his hand.

He opened a drawer, first freeing the thumb and forefinger of his right hand by pressing the stem of the glass against his palm with the lesser fingers, and abstracted a hooded, pullover-style alpaca jerkin – a garment whose design, not least in a line of tasselling on the arm and shoulder, gestured lightly towards the merciless leagues of the Pampas, to feats of horsemanship and endurance, to the unspeakable melancholy of the wind in the innumerable grass.

He found a sleeve and introduced his left arm. Then, and at the same time transferring the glass to his left hand and discovering the other sleeve with his right, he turned and began to cancel the few paces by which he had relinquished his viewpoint. When both hands were free he sighed comfortably, raised his arms, and plunged his head into the main cavity of the garment. Mindful of the ledge, and now no more than a step or two from it, he first made a precautionary halt.

His head, however, found only darkness and the taut containment of the fabric. He tried to squirm through to the other opening, his arms, as though to sweep away the unforeseen imprisonment, making alternate broad movements – so satirising, no doubt coincidentally, certain novice swimmers. Then he felt his head break free and felt cool air on the back of his neck – but his face was still covered. At first puzzled, he quickly realized that he was looking into the hood – that he had put the jerkin on back-to-front.

Alert to the absurdity of his position (he pictured his neighbour across the street, a man, he recalled, somewhat given to raucous humour, watching him with a keen and growing interest) he made what he took to be an about turn and hurriedly sought to resolve the difficulty. He extricated one arm from its sleeve, afterwards making an attempt to dispose of the glass (whose continuing presence, indeed, he found a little puzzling). But his exploratory groping did not find the window ledge; and so, with certain muffled remarks, he transferred the glass to the hand that now protruded from the bottom of the jerkin and, with a considerable effort, disentangled the other arm.

Destiny, who knows your teeming immensity? The grandeur of your calculations? Who can number the paths that divide before our every step? Ignatiez, doubling both arms within the body of the jerkin, attempted to rotate it. In the continuing absence of vision, and momentarily unsure whether it was the jerkin that was rotating or himself, he became dizzy and stumbled backwards. As he twisted to regain his balance he felt a powerful blow on the side of his thigh which he realised, as he toppled over it, to have been inflicted by the window ledge, the reappearance of which thus brought his efforts to a premature and disappointing close.

Little space need be given to speculation on the thoughts our hero may have allowed himself as, trussed in the jerkin and still firmly grasping the wine glass, he made the brief and impetuous journey that followed. Perhaps some reflections, forgivably trite and rueful, on the unsearchable vicissitudes of fate; or a sudden fascination with a turn in the melody of the street sweeper, whose song, as though a shadow of it, would share an ending with his own more copious existence; or perhaps he recalled skipping stones, alone at dusk, on a plaza in the Brazilian quarter of Buenos Aires, in a year of floods and innocence.

III

The pain of writing, whatever the general voice, lies not in starting but in finishing. The phrase that was coined in a balm of self-satisfaction sounds out like a cracked bell; the conceits are wooden, the facetiousness embarrassing; everywhere an odour of thesaurus.

And yet it is all insidiously addictive: the prolix and layered subordinate clauses, the shifting and ironized voicing, the elliptical but priggishly precise adjectives. Has Borges infiltrated such style as I had? And will that colonisation proceed? My fate, to be no more than a thick-tongued puppet of the dead master?

And what of Ginnie? I see her, perhaps, in a Mediterranean setting, the apricot softness of her skin supplanted by the fried-chicken gloss of tanned middle age, her now crabbed toes still revealed by sandals, their nails still defiantly painted. She sits with eyes closed and with a slight and introspective smile; a fat and genial man, perhaps her husband, hums quietly as he busies himself with some small task in the background.

That smile – did she scatter the seeds of stories to her many lovers, with ingenious hints tailored to each one's quirks and enthusiasms? And does she wait, with patient assurance, for the fruits of that sowing to find their way to her across the unforgivable decades, like love-gifts, like accolades?

Leaving The Island

George McKissock

The rain lay like a blanket over the island. We get quite a few days like this in early summer. The mist comes down over everything till you can barely distinguish sea from land, or the stretch of road in front of you. Weather like this is dangerous for cyclists. Everyone tends to drive too fast in bad weather, often without lights. Some locals are just as bad as the tourists. Foreigners are the worst though, as they often forget what side they're supposed to be driving on. Mind you, with some of the narrow roads around here, it doesn't make much difference. I always have my lights on in weather like this. It makes good sense to depend on listening rather than looking when the weather's like this. Luckily, it's not too far to the shop from here. Today, I could hear the larks singing through the milkiness above. I don't know how they find their nests again.

I got a bottle of wine today, and other bits and pieces. I'm down at the shop quite a bit, what with one thing and another. I keep a good stock of tinned and dried food in the house of course, but for the likes of bread and milk, fruit, veg and of course the paper, I go to the shop. It's either Betty or Anna who'll serve me, so I get all the news as well as my shopping. It's a kind of place which sells just about everything; it has to, as it's the only one in the village, down by the pier. It's not laid out very well, unlike some others I've been in, more like a storeroom. But once you get used to where things are it's no bother. The tourists get right confused, of course. Mind you, Betty or Anna are right helpful if you can't find anything. They can nearly always lay a hand on whatever you want.

I trimmed my beard today. I've been meaning to do it for some time. I always let it grow longer in the winter to protect my face a bit. I'm out with the sheep in the worst of weathers. The wind's the worst: it drives rain, snow or hail through all your layers. I could use a haircut as well. I cut my own after old Jock died, but it's not the same. There's a lass does hair in the village now, ladies and gents. I feel awkward about having my hair cut by a woman. Still, there's no other choice really. During the lambing, I tend to let myself go a bit. I'm out day and night, and just grab a bite and a wash when I can. I look after the poorly ones in the byre so I can tend them easily. It's good to see a wee thing getting stronger when you doubted it would ever make it. Anyway, like I say, I'm getting it a bit easier, so I can start paying a bit of attention to myself and the house. It's the same every year. Once the worst of the lambing is over, I catch up on my sleep, then the house, then myself. There are other reasons I've started paying attention to myself, too.

I'm not down at the shop much during lambing, so I tend to run out of things. I get by, nonetheless. With not going down, I miss other things as well. I lose touch with what's happening on the island. All the scandal and gossip. I'm so busy at the time I don't give it a thought. I get totally lost in my battle to save as many lambs and ewes as I can. Most times, the enemy is the weather. I'm so tired, I sometimes fall asleep undressed, sometimes in the chair. However, once I go back down the shop again I always find there's a lot to catch up on. I feel like Rip Van Winkle. However, this year has been different in a number of ways. For the first time I've not had to rely on the shop for all my news. In fact, for the first time, I've probably been part of that news.

It's hard to say where it all began, at least where I was concerned. On the hill or in the shop. Take your pick. I'd seen them on the hill, hand in hand, and seen his car on the droveroad through my binoculars. But it was really the shop which brought me my lodger. It was alive with speculation about the affair; the whole place crawled with it. Rachael was a farmer's wife from the shieling on the other side of the island, Graham worked for a feed stock company on the mainland. It wasn't that big a surprise. For years before one of the regular pieces of news was the way Davie treated his wife. Drunk Davie he was known as. He was a bit shy, but hard working right enough. But he was a cruel man when he was drunk. He was often drunk. Then she'd be in the shop trying to cover up her bruises with stories about falling over. I saw her twice like that myself, trying to make jokes about being "accident prone". She was being that brave I wanted to go and hug her. I didn't, of course. When she was younger, her parents still lived down the road and she would come by to help me with the lambing. She was good, careful and gentle. We got on fine. She had a great sense of humour then. She could even make me laugh. Davie knocked it all out of her. I saw her shrink into herself, become neglectful, hopeless. I could do nothing of course. Until that day.

One of my rare visits at the beginning of lambing. I'd run out of oatcakes and I needed a big supply as I never bothered with bread around then. It went stale too quickly. I knew something was wrong as soon as I walked into the shop. They were standing in a huddle in the corner, Rachael, Betty and Anna. Rachael was crying sore, and Anna's arms were wrapped round her. I'd have gone back out if I hadn't needed the oatcakes. I hadn't the time to come back again. Betty came over to me. "She's left him," she said, her eyes shining with the excitement of it all. "He's given her her last hammering," she added fiercely as she disappeared into the back shop. She hadn't asked me what I wanted. She came back out with a pot of tea and four cups. "Here," she said to Rachael. "strong and sweet, it'll do you good." Anna fetched her a chair and Rachael sat down. She seemed calmer now. I relaxed a little. I'm useless with tears. Betty thrust a cup at me. I took it, speechless. In all the years I'd been a customer I've never had so much as an extra sweetie in the bag, let alone a cup of tea. "Where will you stay?" Anna was asking gently, crouching down beside her. Rachael shook her head, letting loose more tears. I looked away. Her parents lived with her sister in Inverness.

"She can stay with me," I looked round to see who had spoken then realised it was me. I'd been remembering how she was, and seeing her like this made me angry. All the same … Betty obviously agreed, "Well, that's kind of you, Willie, but maybe it's not a very good idea. You a single man and all." She was right, of course. But I knew that neither she and George nor Anna and her mother had room. Rachael had no family on the island. I couldn't bear the thought of her begging at doors to be taken in. She was too good for that. Her head was down and her shoulders were shaking gently. I couldn't bear it. Like something possessed, I went over to her and crouched by her like Anna had done. I put my hand on her shoulder till she looked up at me. Her face had a livid, swollen mark obscuring her right cheekbone, and her eyes were red with crying. I remembered the little girl who'd cried when a lamb had died. "You're coming home with me," I told her. I was not the only one shocked by my boldness. Anna was looking at me as if I was a stranger. And in the background Betty was saying "Well, really …" Rachael simply nodded. I picked up her case, slung it across the bike, and we walked back up the road in silence. Only when we reached the house did I realise I'd forgotten the oatcakes.

Rachael's stay lasted over two months. The spare room had to be cleared out, of course. With her helping me, it didn't take long. Most of the stuff's in the byre, where it should have been from the start. We got on fine, though it was strange having someone other than Rory about the place. There were a few changes around the house. I had an assistant for the lambing, and cooked meals into the bargain. I didn't ask any questions of her. I was as happy with her being silent as not. When she spoke, I just listened. Conversation is not my strong point. She spent a fair bit of time with Rory, and got fresh things for me from the shop. Rory was stunned by all the attention, and seemed to turn into a puppy again when she was around. I think she hated going to the shop. Knowing she was the main topic of conversation, I mean. But she never showed it.

I didn't notice much change in folk's attitude. Betty still seems overcome by the whole thing, and George even put in an appearance one day with an invitation to go fishing. I made an excuse. Anna once said it was good of me to take Rachael in. I got very embarrassed and tongue-tied. She came to visit us a few times, bringing home-baking, and sometimes flowers. She'd never been in my house since we were kids at school together. These were good times. I think she was surprised I didn't live in a greater muddle. Mind you, most of the credit was due to Rachael. When Anna visited they spent a lot of time talking together. When I was in, we'd all relax in front of the fire. It felt good to have conversation in the house again, without needing to contribute to it. Davie came round one night. He never got beyond the door. I thought about picking up my gun, but I needn't have worried. Rory was snarling and growling to get at him, so he didn't hang around. Rachael was quite upset, and I wished that Anna had been there. She made a big fuss of Rory. Davie never came back.

Most weekends Graham was over. I seldom saw them, but I didn't mind. With him, she was the way I remembered her. He brought plenty of free 'samples', and fixed my radio one day. Sometimes at night we'd share a bottle of Malt he'd bring, and talk about the future of farming. We weren't optimistic, and Rachael would scold us for being so gloomy. She was quite relaxed with him in front of me, as if she'd wanted me to be able to share in her affection for him. I never felt shut out. It was a whole new routine for me, and the time passed so quickly. It was a good lambing, I didn't lose many lambs, and no ewes at all. As Spring gave way to Summer, I was aware that other changes were due. They spent a lot of time talking about the future. It was finally decided.

They're leaving today. Graham arrived yesterday, and they went round to get more of her things. I offered him my gun, but he didn't take it. There was no trouble; Davie wasn't around. They offered me a lift to the ferry in the car, but I cycled down instead. There wasn't much room, and it saved me walking back. They stopped at the shop on the way down; I think to thank Anna and to say goodbye. I peddled on through the mist to the pier. There was only old Sandy and a couple of hikers from the hostel there. A stray dog was sniffing the creels. Gulls came and went, silently piercing the haar. I could hear the throb of the ferry through the gloom. They'd have to hurry. She was unloading by the time they arrived; four cars and a minibus. The first swallows of the summer season. Rachael got out while Graham took the car on. She'd no words left. I did well: I was able to joke with her about the mess Rory and I would soon be in. She laughed though there were tears in her eyes. Graham shook my hand, and slipped an arm around her waist. As they walked on to the ramp, Rachael turned and ran back. "I forgot," she said. "Anna gave me a message for you. She'd like you to come out for a meal." She kissed my cheek. I could smell her perfume. Then she was gone.

They stood on deck, looking back as the boat was swallowed up by the mist. I didn't need binoculars to see her face had crumpled. But though I stood and watched till long after they'd gone from sight, I was somewhere else. A year after Ronnie was killed, I wrote to Anna. She never replied. After that, she was always a little distant with me. We were closer when he'd been alive. Both through our school days and even after she got married. And now this. I couldn't understand it. I cycled back in a trance, only waking up when I almost collided with the postie's van. I didn't know what to do about the invitation. It was another complication in my life. Mind you, the last one hadn't turned out so badly. Perhaps it was time to develop this reputation of mine. A slight breeze got up, and started to clear the mist.

Reviews

Clann Ruaraidh

Meall Garbh/The Rugged Mountain, Ruaraidh MacThòmais/Derick Thomson, Gairm, £7.50; *Fon t-Slige/Under the Shell*, Anne Frater, Gairm, £6.60; *A' Gabhail Ris*, Maoilios M Caimbeul, Gairm, £6.60; *Scotland o Gael an Lawlander*, Derrick McClure et al., Gairm, £7.50.

The publishers Gairm was established by Derick Thomson and Finlay J MacDonald in 1951 and has ever since published a wide selection of creative, educational and academic literature in Gaelic, both contemporary and ancient, as well as a quarterly magazine, also entitled *Gairm*. Finlay J MacDonald died in 1987, but the publishing firm and magazine still flourish under Derick Thomson.

Gairm has, notably, published most of the best verse in Gaelic in the last fifty years. I say most because, for reasons rendered largely irrelevant by death, it has not published that of the late Sorley MacLean (apart from one or two poems in early numbers of the magazine). *Meall Garbh/The Rugged Mountain* is the sixth individual collection of poems by Derick Thomson. Its concerns are unsurprising: Scottish and Gaelic topography, history and politics and the poet's relationship with the community, cultural and spatial, to which he belongs. The tone of delivery or utterance varies throughout: he is jocular in, for example, 'A' Togail Dhealbh'/ 'Taking Photographs':

Cailleach mhòr Shasannach
is briogais teann oirr',
air màs man tuba,
a' togail dhealbh de tharbh Gaidhealach ...
Cha robh fhios aice dè chanadh i
nuair a thug an tarbh/Leica às a dhosan
's a thog e dealbh/dhith fhèin.

(A large English lady/wearing tight slacks,
her bottom like a tub,
taking photographs
of a Highland bull ...
She didn't know what to say
when the bull
took a Leica from his forelock
and took a snap of her.)

That made me laugh (and not just because it reminded me of an Irish joke). Satire – in the modern sense – is employed in poems such as 'Cridhe na h-Alba'/ 'The Heart of Scotland', with less effect than direct humour. The poet is at his most considered when addressing polemical issues, not least of which is the decay of the Gaelic language and all it represents, corresponding it seems to his own personal decay (if that's the word for what is, after all, a natural process). This manifests itself in a wholly characteristic admixture of despondency and hope, but with a certain magnanimity of vision and acceptance which was unexpected. The title poem is, in fact, a sequence written in 1988, recalling a family holiday in Perthshire in the 1930's, with a powerful resonance, both personally and to the linguistic community.

Thomson's poetry is at its best when it is free from distracting devices and abstractions, as in the poem in this collection entitled 'Rùsgadh'/ 'Baring', concerning a reformed elder of the Free Church:

… corra uair, nuair a bheir thu sùil
air an ta-tù ud
thig rudan neònach gu do chuimhne,
boillsgeadh de Shingapore's de Hong Kong
mus do chuir thu eòlas air a' Chruthaighear.

(Occasionally, when your eye falls
on the tattoo
odd things come to mind,
a glimpse of Singapore and of Hong Kong
before you got to know the Creator.)

Derick Thomson was born and reared in Payble, Lewis, where Anne Frater was born in 1967. Like Thomson, she is an academic – having studied under him at the University of Glasgow before his retirement – and a poet, and her first collection has now been published by Gairm and, indeed, her work echoes her admiration for the work of the older poet. Anne Frater is a political poet, committing a consideration of political issues to verse – and her political conviction is, again, like Thomson, Scottish (and Gaelic) nationalism. Her work, however, reflects other concerns: isolation, love, homeland and feminism. This is neatly itemized in the different sections of the book, which are entitled in a sort of index or, even, a caveat: Thoughts and Sketches; Unrequited and Never Was; Land and Language; People and Places, all of which reminds me that Thomson's first collection was similarly sectionalized. Anne Frater uses natural imagery and language and employs a delicate irony.

The tone of utterance is invariably direct. It is salutary to have in published form poetry in Gaelic written by young native speakers.

A' Gabhail Ris, the fourth collection by Myles Campbell (to use the Anglicized form of his name) is in Gaelic only, which may be both limiting and enhancing. The influence of the society to which he belongs, in terms of language and religion, is addressed or simply appears, time and again. Like all the best Gaelic poets he rejects dogma with a vigour. He is a philosophical poet, not alone in the sense that he is prone to speculation, but also that he seems disposed to a considered acceptance of things. It is not clear if that philosophy can be communicated through poetry, or, I should say, into poetry, but Campbell's uncertainties are impressive. The final section of the book consists of a poem in ten sections entitled 'Agus mar sin Car' Mhuiltein'/'And so a Somersault' but it is represented in a sort of prose form which is visually repulsive.

Poems by Myles Campbell are featured in *Scotland o Gael an Lawlander* with others, by Derick Thomson, Donald MacAulay and Aonghas MacNeacail, selected and translated into a synthetic Scots by Derick McClure at the University of Aberdeen. McClure has described himself, with characteristic modesty, as being "sufficiently well-acquainted with Gaelic" to attempt this particular project and the result is extremely pleasing. It certainly represents a useful, if limited, linguistic and literary exercise but it is not to be considered as anything other than a personal selection (which, however, is steadily increasing, as the editor has recently been rendering poems by Meg Bateman, Rody Gorman and Sorley MacLean). The translations from MacLean's work will complement those made by Douglas Young which appeared as part of the collection *Auntran Blads* which appeared in the same year, and from the same publisher, as *Dàin do Eimhir* (1943). The work also extends the general canon of Gaelic verse as rendered into Scots – particularly of the work by George Campbell Hay (Deòrsa Mac Iain Deòrsa), William Neill (Uilleam Nèill) and, most recently, Sheena Blackhall (Sìne NicTheàrlaich). McClure has retained rhythm and raciness and there is a useful glossary appended to the book.

Rody Gorman

Small is Beautiful

Nation and Identity in Contemporary Europe, Brian Jenkins and Spyros A Sofos (eds), Routledge; *The Future of The Nation State*, Sverker Gustavsson and Leif Lewin (eds), Routledge; *The Lesson of This Century*, Karl Popper, Routledge.

At this important stage in our affairs you might expect that new books on the future of the nation state, popular sovereignty and cultural diversity would consider the Scottish case. After all, Scotland has been a pioneer in the evolution of ideas on these subjects and we have just reached a decisive turning point in our constitutional history after more than a hundred years of effort. As far as these books are concerned, Scotland does not exist. Of course Scotland lost control over its foreign policy and its international identity when Jamie the Saxt flitted to London in 1603. That made Scotland officially invisible on the international stage. These books are proof of that invisibility.

The only reference to Scotland occurs incidentally in a paper, "Reconsidering Britishness", by Kenneth Lunn of the University of Portsmouth in *Nation and Identity in Contemporary Europe*. He begins (I was about to add inevitably) with a reference to that English obsession, cricket, and he explains that "non-English" players are those "born outside Britain or who were of Commonwealth descent". This appears to mean that he regards the Scots (and Welsh, Irish, etc.) as English. Of course, we are familiar with the apparent English inability to distinguish between English and British and their habit of using the words interchangeably in both directions. Lunn does this throughout his paper and this reduces much of it to confusion because it is never quite clear when he means England and when he means Britain. In Scotland we assume that this sort of confusion is due to mental laziness or simple ignorance. Lunn however (and this is his only direct reference to Scotland) denies this and tells us in effect that it is a deliberate assertion of English domination. I think that this is often suspected, but I do not remember seeing before such a blunt admission of it. The following is a passage which I think deserves wide circulation because its implications are far-reaching. It is a rude exposure of the con trick which is Britain:

The use of the term 'English' as a synonym for 'British' is more than just a slovenly application of the word. It represents a series of assumptions about the natural right of England to speak for Britain and, by the imposed silence, the inability of Welsh, Irish and Scottish voices to challenge effectively these assumptions. It reproduces the imperial philosophy in which the mother country represented the greater whole.

Perhaps we should expect little attention to Scotland from a book which is the product of a research group in the University of Portsmouth because of the curious blindness of the English (many of them at least) to everything north of the Tweed. How do we fare in *The Future of the Nation State* which consists of papers presented at a symposium at Uppsala University in 1995? Again, Scotland does not appear as a subject, but papers are directed more to general ideas than to particular instances. Many of these ideas have deep roots in Scottish thought. A belief in the virtues of cultural diversity and in the advantages of small over large countries has been expressed by Andrew Fletcher, David Hume, Adam Ferguson, Walter Scott, Hugh MacDiarmid, William McIlvanney and many others. In this book Phillipe Schmitter of Stanford University identities diversity as one of the strengths of Western Europe: "without the preservation of this variety ... Europe would have long since lost its most peculiar comparative advantage." He denies that there is an advantage in size: "small countries are not doing worse than large ones; nor do they seem to be condemned to repeating the policies of their 'superiors'." Indeed some micro states like Andorra, Liechtenstein, Luxembourg, Monaco and San Marino have been remarkably successful. Similarly, Johan Olsen of the University of Oslo remarks that many small European states have a good historical record in democratic development, prosperity and equality. They are more adaptable than larger countries and have a stronger feeling of community, internal stability and external flexibility.

The general conclusion is that the idea that the nation state is dead is highly premature. Gert Hofstede of the University of Limburg points to the remarkable durability of cultural distinctiveness:

two thousand years of history have not wiped out the differences in mentality between peoples once under Rome and those whose ancestors remained barbarians.

Where does this leave Scotland? We were inside the Empire only partly, precariously, and for a short time. On the other hand our education and much of our thought and literature were strongly influenced by classical Rome, and to a lesser extent Greece, for centuries. George Buchanan wrote a definitive work in the 16th century on the Scottish doctrine of the sovereignty of the people, but he wrote it in Latin. The memorial window to him in Greyfriars' in Edinburgh says, in Latin, that Scotland marked the extremity of the Roman Empire, but that it was also the last refuge of Roman eloquence. Perhaps that is the explanation of the Caledonian Antisyzygy; we have a foot in both camps.

The Lesson of This Century contains two interviews conducted by Giancarlo Bosetti, with Sir Karl Popper in 1991 and 1993, followed by two talks which Popper gave in 1988 and 1989. Although Bosetti does not draw attention to it, there is a marked difference in Popper's opinions between the talks and the interviews. In the talks he says that the West, and particularly Europe, has become "the best and justest world that we know of historically". This is something which we should celebrate, but people grumble and complain "about the terrible world we have to live in". Popper says that spreading such lies is the greatest crime of our age, because it threatens to rob young people of the right to hope and optimism. By 1991, however, Popper takes a much more pessimistic view. After the needs to preserve peace and stop the population explosion, he gives as a priority the need to educate children to curb the decline into violence which has been fostered by television. "If we go on as we do now, we shall soon be living in a society where murder is our daily bread". In just two years the West has changed for Popper from the best and justest society to one where we are imminently threatened by the breakdown of the rule of law and of civilisation itself. Who is robbing us now of our right to optimism?

Paul H Scott

Scotland the Anecdotal

The Ice Horses, The Second Shore Poets Anthology,
Stewart Conn and Ian McDonough (eds), Scottish
Cultural Press, £5.95; *Cabaret McGonagall*, W N
Herbert, Bloodaxe, £7.95; *No Hiding Place*, Tracey
Herd, Bloodaxe, £6.95; *Aphrodite's Anorak*, Hugh
McMillan, Peterloo Poets, £6.95.

In *The Ice Horses*, Ken Cockburn declares:

Poems and dreams too, are stitched
on whatever. thread's at hand
makeshift amalgams of
what's present, remembered, desired.

This is a good description, not of poetry in
general, but of the poetry found in these collections: a poetry of anecdote and of 'identity'
construed as family resemblance and longing.
The ambition of the Shore poets is to promote
'live poetry', 'spoken verse', but it is difficult
to see how such poetry differs from what we
may encounter on the page. And it is better for
that, for, in *The Ice Horses*, we find well-
crafted verse: Gerry Cambridge eking out an
insight into a relationship from an owl crossed
while driving; a kingfisher arousing in Stuart
A Paterson an observation about time; Iain
Crichton Smith stooping to berate the effete
Bonnie Prince Charlie. There is no escaping,
however, the rather limited nature of this
poetry's intellectual scope: Shaun Belcher's
bleating about 'severed tongues'; Brian
McCabe's observation: 'We are the seagulls \
We are the people'. As for Anne C Frater:

Was it better
to just dream of the sweetness
and how it would be,
than to taste the fickle honey of love
and the sting it leaves behind?

Here, flabby sub-sixth-form threnodies are
accorded cultural capital by the simple fact of
being written in Gaelic.

Hugh McMillan is described on the cover
of *Aphrodite's Anorak* as being 'savagely
funny', but there is little here to prove that,
especially the facetiously scatological 'Letter
from the 24th Congress of the Communist
Party' (Paul Durcan has satirised this much
more effectively). McMillan is instead a good,
observant poet, with an eye for his native
Dumfries and Galloway. There is the familiar
concern with national identity – 'a country
that is, and isn't'; 'there was a moment, / at the

teeth of it, / when I felt / Scottish' – and a history teacher, healthy scepticism about the heritage industry. The best poem of this
collection is 'Getting too Late for Football',
where a scene of domestic life takes on greater
significance: 'there are still things to do / and
a route to try and find / through the dark'.

The ability to 'make strange' the everyday
(when was it ever not?) is a strength of Tracey
Herd, whose excellently-crafted work offers a
distinct, female perspective on relationships.
As in 'Words of Love': "Your arse and cunt
look like / a butcher's shop, he said / rubbing
his fingers along her bloody crack."
Such concerns could become all-too-human.
Instead, Herd shows a refreshing sensitivity
to what might be called the 'cosmic', as in
'The Snow Storm', where one is struck not
only by the mysterious presence of an
escaped hospital patient, but also the nocturnal winter scene. And in 'Coronach', "The
moon is sheer ice or a cracked watch-face /
that swung on its fragile chain of stars. / Night
is falling at its own modest pace."

There are lots of horses in these collections.
In *The Ice Horses*, the eponymous poem is
typically an occasion for reminiscence about
the patrilinear heritage. Horses are particularly prevalent in Herd's work (a girlish
thing?) where they embody robust, yet
doomed heroism, as in 'The Front-Runner',
the burst heart, bright / as silks, fluttering
briefly / as his rivals take repeated flight.

W N Herbert observes and no doubt identi-
fies with 'A Difficult Horse'. Herbert is
undoubtedly one of the most talented and
vibrant Scottish voices. As far as spoken verse
and humour are concerned, he knocks spots
off these other writers. He displays a talent for
cruel pun and neologism that obviously seeks,
and sometimes manages, to emulate his hero,
Mark E Smith. It is especially when describing crossing the border that Herbert rises to
the linguistic and imaginative challenge, as
'In Chips We Trust' and 'Road Movie': *Kil-
mont Willie and the Melrose Kid; The Good,
The Bad and the Northumbrian*, indeed.
Linked to this is Herbert's concern with Scotland's identity, or lack of it, and feelings of
persecution in the British literary world.

I cannot help but be struck by the discrep-
ancy between Herbert's imaginative energy –

there are moments when, especially in 'Road Movie' and 'Dog Conversion Chart', that the fantasy could go on gloriously forever – and the poverty of the concern with the Scottish nation. Such poetry is too often stuck within the confines of anecdote and 'belonging'. How will the creation of a Scottish Parliament affect the work of Herbert and others like him? I am struck, in all four of these collections, by the anonymity of Capital, which extends its domination behind the multicultural cacophony. Herbert, author of 'The Ballad of Techofear' cannot see technology in the context of the workplace and the environment. So beyond the ingenious posturing in the cultural field, I find refreshing a poem like 'Looking Up From Aeroplanes':

> Do you too soon forget the brown
> frownland far below,
> between the slippery blotchings of
> cloud shadows, the
> zip-fasteners of farm-lanes,
> the telephone pad-hatchings of the towns
> and look up?

Gavin Bowd

Male Persperspective

The Bowels of Christ, Graham Lironi, Black Ace Books, £6.95; *Kill Kill Faster Faster*, Joel Rose, Rebel Inc., £6.99; *Zaire*, Harry Smart, Dedalus, £8.99; *Life on a Dead Planet*, Frank Kuppner, Polygon, £7.99.

Having had a quick look at these four books prior to actually reading them for review, I had naughtily worked out all sort of preconceived notions regarding them, and to serve me right for my arrogance, only one of them turned out to be as I had expected.

Graham Lironi's *The Bowels of Christ* has a recommendation by A L Kennedy, citing the author as 'intelligent, original and disturbing', which in general is true. The work, described as a tale of teenage sex, lies and hill-walking, twists around a few different central characters, who have rather convoluted relationships with each other, and one of whom has the same name as the author. This is apparently to make the reader ask the question "Did this really happen?", but it unfortunately did not have that affect – a few of the events seemed a little implausible (which, of course, is not to say that *none* of it happened).

The whole set-up of events in the book is fascinating, especially with regard to Carol and Carl, the young couple around whom most of the plot is centred. Their relationship is the oddest in the book – no details, since it would ruin part of the action – they are connected by a very strong bond despite being the negative/positive image of each other. After a mountain-climbing accident, Carl makes a decision which has serious repercussions on their lives, and those of their parents, one of whom is thought to be dead. The lives of the parents in their youth is also explored a bit, to provide background for the main story. This works to a certain extent, but while the ideas the book is trying to explore are very interesting and quite different, the length of the novel lets them down – it's really far too short to accomplish what it sets out to achieve. This reads like a synopsis for what should be a deeply investigated and detailed work, which, if it kept the same skill and intelligence all the way through, would probably be quite brilliant. The use of the story of James Nelson running parallel to the main theme was also unimpressive and rather unneccessary.

I really looked forward to reading *Kill Kill Faster Faster* for various reasons, not least of which was Irvine Welsh's comment that "This book is destined to be the classic New York novel … it demands to be picked up and read. Then just try putting it down." It was much more effort trying to be bothered picking it up to be honest.

At first, it read really well, and Joey One-Way, the protagonist seemed to be an incredibly interesting character. A white man who seems to think he's got 'black attitude' and who has been put in jail for murdering his wife (which he can't remember doing), Joey at the beginning of the novel talks of his daughters whom he wants to forgive him. This leads to the assumption that the main plot of the novel would be based around his relationship with his daughters, but shortly after this, the book drops into a story of sex and violence, with the obligatory mention of drugs.

Joey ends up having an affair with a beautiful ex-prostitute who is now married to Joey's new boss. Besides describing the sex he has with Fleur, or 'Flowers', as he calls her (and all the things she loves him to do to her, typically enough – sad male fantasy or what!) Joey also relates how his boss tries it on with him as well, and Rose seems to revel in going into detail about sex in prisons. All this would be acceptable if done in an interesting way, trying to explore reasons for certain actions and attitudes, but when sex is constantly referred to with no real necessity, you really begin to wonder if there was a specific quota the author had to fulfil in order to get a contract, and when the word 'cunt' is used seven times in just over a page, you have to ask if the author's imagination goes no further than general scenarios rather than being sustainable through an entire novel (and it's not even that long at 197 pages). It's a pity that the only factor of real interest, i.e., the daughters, is almost completely ignored when it should be explored much deeper than Joey seeing them for the first time as adults, and being unable to talk to them because they are beautiful women instead of children. Recommended only for those heavily into novels centred around sex, crimes and violence.

A novel that doesn't feel the need to rely on pathetic sex scenes to interest readers is *Zaire*, by Harry Smart. This was the book mentioned earlier which is exactly what it first seems to be – interesting, intelligent, full of suspense. Set in London and Zaire, the principal player in the political game is Philippe, who is torn between his position in working for the Zairean Security Service and protecting his wife and son, and trying to make peace with himself over events that his actions have brought about, both directly and indirectly. Like Lironi's book, *Zaire* calls on the past to explain present situations, and like Rose's, it utilises violence to bring home certain points. *Unlike* the other two books, though, there is subtlety here, particularly with respect to the violent acts that are committed, and they completely justify themselves by illustrating the reality of the situation, and the real danger which Philippe has placed himself and his family in by wanting to play things his own way.

Every time the wife was mentioned, it seemed certain that she was going to die, or that something else horrendous was going to happen to her. This almost overpowers the wider political issues, but they are still nonetheless gripping, even for someone who knows absolutely nothing about African politics. This mix of politics, intrigue and human concern definitely makes this the best of this selection.

Last, but not least, Frank Kuppner's *Life on a Dead Planet* has another slightly odd scenario – it focuses on the narrator wandering through a city at night and imagining what goes on in other peoples lives, trying to connect things which one might not normally associate as having a relationship of any significant kind. This novel forcibly pulls the reader into the story. The first few pages aren't enthralling, but the reader is soon hooked on the philosophies. On page thirty-seven it is obvious that the reader is onto a good thing when the sentence "I am trying to describe life, you unutterable half-wits" is directed at them. Kuppner obviously has a sense of humour. And a bizarre train of thought – from seeing windows containing vases, cats, etc. the narrator realises no people are looking out, and decides that "everyone, apparently, was killing his husband or wife by devious means in one of the back rooms. Probably by poison. A curious business indeed. Don't eat that cake!" The only slight drawback to this work is that any plot apparently is simply a pretext for the the author's personal musings, but it's interesting enough to be excused and it's very thought-provoking as well.

C J Lindsay

Theatre Roundup

My first Festival had a definite literary feel to it. Not knowing where to begin when choosing shows I went for names I recognised and enjoyed; Shakespeare, Joyce, Elliot, Kerouac and ended up with an eclectic mix of literary biographies and the authors' own works.

Bye Bye Blackbird, playing at the Assembly Rooms, is a one woman show written by Willard Simms with Beth Fitzgerald vivaciously playing Zelda Fitzgerald, wife of the novelist F. Scott. The text mixes anecdotes of her life in high society Paris and New York in the 1920s and 30s, with her desires for her own success and identity away from her husband and tops it off with moments of frightening obsession. Fitzgerald handled these intense emotions with panache while being an exemplar hostess, entertaining the audience with tales of her husband, Hemingway and Gertrude Stein. These episodes also reveal her jealousy of their independence and her hatred for the way they treated her. The sparse scenery of a bed allowed Fitzgerald to keep the spotlight on herself as Zelda was never able to in her own life.

In the Nottingham Playhouse's performance at the King's Theatre of *Measure for Measure* directed by Stephane Braunschweig, the scenery was the only star. A huge construction of several levels of sliding walls that swiveled around to a clashing heavy rock track it had much more presence than any of the actors. The members of the cast moved through the play with a solid, professional approach, but there was no one character that sets himself apart. Even the comic players David Sapani and Tony Cownie seemed too accomplished to enjoy their parts.

Brian McMaster has always ploughed his own furrow as far as the commissioning of Scottish work for the official festival is concerned. One of his great successes last year was the *Songs of the North East* series, celebrating its rich oral tradition. This year it was the Gaels' turn in the wonderful series of con-

certs, *The Song of the Gael* – a glorious celebration of a literary and musical tradition born on the periphery of Europe, yet one of the greatest triumphs of Western Culture.

Each concert was packed, both audience-wise and in the programme on offer. Each concert focused on a different aspect of Gaelic music and song: *The Cave of Gold* demonstrated the intimate connection between Gaelic song and the music of the pipes; *The Song of the Seasons* showed the influence of the external factors of changing seasons, landscape, climate on the culture it produces, *Scotland and Ireland* linked together these two main tributaries of the Gaelic stream and there was an informal ceilidh to provide a flavour of that age-old custom of the visit, where people foregather, by intent or accident, and the inevitable happens: song, story, music and fun.

It is an invidious and perhaps erroneous exercise to single out from this series of concerts particular highlights: performances of course varied, but there was so much of the highest quality. However, I'm going to indulge myself. In the singing there was Mary Smith's 'Tri Fichead Bliadhna', a song composed by her great grandfather lamenting a brother's exile in Canada, both separated forever by the fact that neither could read or write – sung with utter authority and poise; also unforgettable was 'The Eternal Sense of the Sea' sung by Ishbel MacAskill and Mary Stewart with 'I Will Lift Up My Pipe. Amongst the music there was a feast of skill on display, but, not surprisingly, the piping stood out, notably from the brothers Angus and Iain MacDonald.

Linked to this enterprise was the ecumenical church service to mark the 1400th anniversary of St Columba's coming to Scotland. Faultlessly organised by Kenna Campbell, the service celebrated in music and song the influence of Columba, potent to this day. But I will never forget the words of Professor Donald MacLeod, giving the sermon, who gave Columba's mission a very modern emphasis: "Let us move beyond defending ourselves, let's move beyond apology. Here, on the edge, we can see and listen. But from here, too, we proclaim and persuade." Columba was also remembered in Iain Crichton Smith's excellent play *Colum Cille* (Stray Theatre) at the

Famous Grouse House, in which I witnessed one of the most memorable performances by a youngster I've ever seen: Georgie Sutton as the young Columba.

Also the Grouse House, *The Merchant of Venice* directed by Edward Argent of Prime Productions was faster paced, though a little rough at the edges. The actors managed to keep even the school students in the audience entertained. Michael Perceval-Maxwell played the comic character with energy and tongue set firmly in cheek while the rest of the cast seemed to relish their roles. Set in the present day with the actors in suits and ties and boilersuits carrying mobile phones, the themes of the 1690s were well translated.

Timeless devised by David Greig of Suspect Culture at the Gateway Theatre combines four characters each with a set of simple repetitious movements, representing their personalities with a simple story and elegant music. Broken into three parts (the present, past and how the characters would like their lives to be) the piece was one section too long. The music was more moving than the performers who had to drag themselves and the audience through the endless reiteration of their characters' fears and nervous twitches. In the last section the lines repeated over and over again began to grate on the nerves and the audience began to chant with the actors in a sort of desperation to have the whole thing over with.

Written by Kathryn Willsteed, *Anäis Anagram*, based on the diaries of Anäis Nin, deals with the subject of her incestuous relationship with her father. The setting of the one woman play was almost too intimate. The play was held in a damp basement room in a building a few doors away from the main Demarco European Art Foundation which was cold and uncomfortable for both performer (obvious from the sweater she threw on soon after the applause) and audience. Roberta Lemon played the strong Nin and sat only yards away from the audience and rarely looked away, deliberately trying to shock with her total refusal to take a moral stance on her behaviour. But the half hour only allowed the play to graze the psychological and literary impact of the affair for Nin. Ideas were simply thrown out, leaving the audience emotionally exhausted. The actress did the best she could with the mis-

erable setting as she tried to connect with the audience, but the script dis not allow her to confront her demons as elegantly as the diary text demands.

Theatre Cryptic's *Parallel Lines* was a pure treat. In its second year at the Fringe Festival, this year at the Famous Grouse House, it remained fresh and innovative and deserves another mention. The stunning interposition of James Joyce's stream-of-consciousness text with song and music was carried out with the erotic vitality and energy of the original text. Four women played Molly Bloom; an actress, a singer and two musicians. The scenery was simple but lush including a large bed and later a tank of water in which the actress Molly recited the 'Yes' section of *Ulysses*.

Citylight Productions' performance of *The Kerouac Triangle* at Cafe Graffiti charts the relationship of the epitome of America's Beat Generation; author of *On the Road*, Jack Kerouac, his fast living side-kick Neil Cassady and their lover and wife Carolyn Cassady, the surviving member of the trio. The play written by Vivien Devlin uses Carolyn's memoirs as a foundation and once again there is a mixing of media here. Kerouac's jazz poetry style is used in the dialogue, photographs, words and abstract designs were flashed up onto a wall and jazz music was occasionally played. But all the poetry was lost in the actors' attempts to recapture the fire and darkness of this relationship. A horrid rendition of Allen Ginsberg's poem of a generation 'Howl' only increased the insult. Marcus MacLeod played Kerouac with a forced accent (possibly too close to reality) which was distracting as it made the rhythms Kerouac was known for hard to follow. All this aside, the play is an intriguing look into the loves in Kerouac's life; Carolyn, jazz music, life on the road and his writing.

The Royal Lyceum Theatre Company's performance of T S Elliot's *The Cocktail Party* celebrates fifty years of Elliot's plays at the Festival. Starring some well-known faces from television, Simon Jones, David Bamber and Maggie Steed, it was surprisingly bland. The highlights are Steed as Julia who burst into every scene and kept the audience giggling at her nosey attempts to push the characters into action and Clive Merrison as Harcourt-Reilly who was sinister and crafty in

the first scene and all-knowing and sympathetic in the rest of the play. Bamber was not convincing, uncertain whether to be pathetic or decisive. The reunion of the couple was unbelievable but this could partly be Elliot's script which tried to deal with his own guilt over his treatment of his wife whom he had institutionalised and his unfulfilled American lover.

And finally for a little poetic comedy, Jill Peacock and Viv Gee in *Burns Baby Burns* mixed their own topical poetry with their insights on the state of the world and their own lives. They dealt well with a power failure early in the show, delivering wit, dance, change costumes and jumping around the stage and at the audience at break-neck speed. A enjoyable change from high theatre and polished actors Peacock and Gee are down-to-earth, alternative and fun as they look at everyday subjects in an 'at the pub with your mates on a drunken Sunday afternoon' way.

Gerry Stewart

Pamphleteer

Headland Publications (38 York Avenue, West Kirby, Wirral, Merseyside L48 3JF) offer an interesting selection which should entertain through the long winter nights. There is a decidedly European influence, with a wide range of views and insights from poets Mario Petrucci, Roger Elkin and John Greening. The pick of the bunch has to be Petrucci's *Shrapnel and Sheets (£6.95)*, the title itself indicating the dichotomous aspect of his work. His kaleidoscopic vision of humanity flits from the personal to the political, from the tragic to the ironic, in an almost effortless way. In 'Latitudes', we see the poet gazing across the globe as he moves from Hanah, a girl in Abadan, who "... Steps on a landmine – for one eternal instant sees all the roofs of her village." – to an expectant mother in a New York apartment who "... plays Mozart through a stethoscope to her unborn child." The poet's perspective is often blunt and necessarily harrowing (in 'The Confession of Borislav Herlak' we hear the monologue of a Sarajevo war criminal describing the brutal butchering of Moslems), but always human, always reminding us of things we should never forget.

A bit gentler is Roger Elkin's *Points of Reference (£6.95)*. His poetry is skilful and erudite, and although it doesn't reach the emotional heights of Petrucci's work, it has clear values of its own. The language is sharp and observational, and succeeds in raising the quotidian to poetic realms. We share a true sense of the bustle of the French market place in 'Game Market, Neuborg, Normandy', as the poet describes cages packed with live birds, wives haggling over the price of hens, and the deluge of straw and feathers left behind. We share in the poet's sense of wonder at it all, and think of our own clinical supermarkets, where we buy sanitised slabs of chicken from chilled counters, without a second thought of the animal itself. This cultural disparity is something that the poet highlights nicely; French farmers are "tied to history", while he, like us, claims "true twentieth century anonymity". The final section of the book, reflecting the poet's visit to Istria (a region of the former Yugoslavia not yet embroiled in war) is a dark, worthy portrayal of a people struggling against poverty and the greed of capitalism which threatens to destroy the traditional way of life.

John Greening's new collection, *The Coastal Path* (£6.95) is an interesting read. His poetry is lyrical and steeped in historicism, but it felt like the kind of poetry that tends to float over one's head rather than leave a lasting impression.

Anyone with an interest in the Welsh myths of the Mabinogion, should certainly take a look at another Headland publication, *Gronw's Stone: Voices from the Mabinogion* (£6.95) by Ann Gray and Edmund Cusick. The four branches of the Mabinogi are the most famous of the medieval Celtic stories, and are a merging of Welsh mythology, folklore and Arthurian romance. For those not familiar with the stories, the book gives an outline of each branch before you embark on the poetic monologues of various characters, who lament their troubles and express their fears and desires. The language is rich and erotic, reflecting the inspiration gained by the poets from the original text. Also worth a mention are the fine illustrations by Margaret Jones which help to bring the poems to life. Overall, a fresh and evocative read for old hands and beginners alike.

Headland's final offering is *The Poet's View: Poems for Paintings in the Walker Art Gallery, Liverpool.* (£10.95), compiled and edited by Gladys Mary Coles. Inspired by the wide range of art on display at the Liverpool gallery, the editor arranged a number of workshops on poetry and art, the best of the results appearing in this anthology. The book is beautifully compiled with vibrant reproductions of paintings ranging from Edgar Degas' 'Woman Ironing' (accompanied by Seamus Heaney's 'Old Smothering Iron') to Holbein's 'Portrait of Henry VIII'. What makes the book a real pleasure is the unpretentious variety of the work included – Coles' anthology has work by pupils from the local secondary schools, as well as well-known poets. The result is an interesting and inspired collection, and a delightful book to dip in to.

From art and poetry to science and poetry in Diana Syder's *Hubble* (Smith/Doorstop Books, The Poetry Business, The Studio, Byram Arcade, Westgate, Huddersfield HD1 1ND £5.95). The poet's preoccupation with humanity's interaction with the wider universe goes back to Donne and the metaphysical poets, but a poetic celebration of technology is not a common theme in modern poetry. So after opening the book with a sense of excitement, *Hubble's* contents were a disappointment. Not that Syder doesn't present some interesting ideas – it just comes across as a very low-key affair. 'Figures on a Hill' is an interesting study of the different perspectives of a musician, mathematician, molecular biologist and mountaineer (among others), but what inspired the poet to write 'Walkman' is not quite clear – the 'obedience of the buttons'? Surely not. The affiliation between art and science is never fully explored or understood. Neither does the poet show a scientific understanding of nature. There seems to be little point of writing about something complex in a such superficial way, no matter how innovative the idea.

Also from Smith/Doorstop Books are a number of pamphlets at £2.95 each. *No Theatre* by Jane Draycott, and *Our Childhood Houses* by Rosaleen Croghan are worth a look, as is Sean O'Brien's *Ideology*. John Hilton's *The Full Yard*, is, however, particularly recommended. His poetry has the quirky colloquialism of a Raymond Carver short story – it's full of domestic understatements about dreams unrealised, lives ruined by drink and fags, and wasted on factory floors. His sad, funny image of a drunk getting into a scrap is a perfect example:

In the road, the traffic stopped
he pocketed his false teeth,
hauled his trousers off, wound them
round his head like a lasso;
I've been a Chinaman all
my life, he said …

New from Katabasis (10 St Martin's Close, London NW1 0HR, £6.95) is Arnold Rattenbury's *Living Here*. The poems, often dark and bitter, explore how capitalism has soiled the beauty of the landscape; his voice vacillates between anger and regret, but is always precise and focused. Although written very much from a Socialist perspective, Rattenbury writes more about landscapes than people; his poetry reflects the world we inhabit, rather than the folk who live there. It is a sobering and thoughtful read.

Less impressive is Raymond Tong's *Returning Home* (published by The University of Salzburg Press and available from Drake International Services, Market House, Market Place, Deddington, Oxford OX15 0SF, £7.95) The tone of these poems is very off-putting – the author's vision seems more patriotic than poetic, and the over-simplistic style often smacks of nursery rhymes. Although the poet's attempt to explain his idea of poetic truth in the introduction is commendable, when he states "England has always played a considerable part in my conception of the truth", his meaning is not clear.

Witch on the Wild Side is a "wee book of poems" by R J Ritchie (published by Paronomaniac Press, c/o Central Action, Unit 22k Thistle Industrial Estate, Stirling FK7 7RZ), and although the price is not evident, it will be donated to Bighearted Scotland, a consortium of Scottish Charities. This is a light-hearted collection, the basis of most poems being a (over) play on words, a barrage of puns. If you like the idea of a poetic version of the World's Worst Jokes, this is the book for you – it'll keep you chuckling into your kipper tie for hours. For a taste of the wit, take this extract from 'Just a Souchong at Twilight.' "… he failed to boil her over and she infused his brew: / "I'm not your China doll, you're not my cup of tea, / leaf off – Ceylon, it's not been good to know you."

Find more fun read-alongs in *A Selection of Modern Traditional Scottish Poems by Donald Dhu* (self-published and available from V Davidson, 49 Main St, Symington, nr. Biggar, S Lanarkshire ML12 6LL). The rhyming is twee – most of the poems read more like songs than verse, and although there didn't seem to be anything particularly modern, traditional, or Scottish about them, they might appeal to someone out there. (Anyone?!)

Neil Rollinson's poems in *A Spillage of Mercury* (Cape Poetry, Random House, 20 Vauxhall Bridge Road, London SW1V 2SA; £7.00) are funny, sexy and irreverent. The author covers a wide spectrum of issues from philosophical fish in 'Descartes', through love, sex, fetishism and other idiosyncrasies, to shopping and religion. Each subject is dealt with both seriously, and in a tongue-in-cheek way (or should that be *seriously tongue-in-cheek?*), and leaves the reader revising former opinions – not always comfortably.

This collection was labelled 'pornography' by one critic, but it's not. The poems simply express truths that lie behind people's natures. Their subjects are unexpected and this may be what shocks some critics; some of the poems revise the relationships between Adam, his first wife Lilith, Eve and God in quite startling and innovative ways! The author also implicates himself quite willingly as being as guilty as anyone else in matters of sex in the last of the poems, 'Blue Movies', in which a half-naked man is found dead in a porn cinema: "The faint scrawl of a name: Robertson, or Rolinston, was pencilled on a cobbler's chit in his trousers" and the similarity to 'Rollinson' is undeniable. Also well-worth mentioning is 'The Miracle of Drink', where Jesus turns water into wine and scotch(!), and He and the disciples "down their drinks in one."

Finally, a children's story – *A Little Girl's Dream* by Shirley Stubbs (Dorrance Publishing, 643 Smithfield St, Pittsburg, Pennsylvania, 15222, £6). This story works on the principle that the dream of every little girl is to be a princess (I thought most kids wanted to be Spice Girls these days). Nothing particularly new or exciting in this bed-time story, although if you know a little girl who likes things pink and fluffy, put this on your Christmas list now.

Emma Pitcairn

Catalogue

This issue's Catalogue rounds up a selection of books mainly concerning the landscape and social history of Scotland. We begin at the end. Ways of death help to define a culture just as much as approaches to life. "This world is a Cite full of streets / And death is the mercat all men meets, / If lyfe were a thing that monie could buy, / The poor would not live and the rich would not die." *Scottish Endings*, edited by Andrew Martin (NMS, £7.99) is one of two recent complementary books about death in all its forms, covering ghosts, murders, epitaphs and executions. Here are stories of funeral feasts and customs, extraordinary burial arrangements and strange discoveries, by, among others, Barrie, Buchan, Burns, Scott and Stevenson. Betty Willsher attempts something similar with *Scottish Epitaphs* (Canongate, £10.99), offering a mix of photographs of gravestones and epitaphs copied from them. The photographs are grainy and atmospheric, of beautiful carved stone images and symbols of angels, death and Father Time. The epitaphs are often poetic and wry, for example :

His mind was weak, his body strong
His answer ready with a song
A mem'ry like him few could boast
Yet suddenly his life was lost.

Stones of all sizes, but natural, not carved, form the subject of two books by David Craig. *Landmarks* (Pimlico, £12.50) is about rocks, crags, mountains, and climbing them. It's also a travel book, written in a discursive style, examining the cultural implications of living in the shadow of large outcrops. *Native Stones* (Pimlico, £10.00) also takes this philosophical approach. Craig is a creative writing teacher as well as a climber. Here he muses on the connections between the act of climbing and the creative use of language.

So much of your time on the rockface is necessarily still, contemplative, alternating with intense spells which plumb your innermost self and make fresh material available to your imagination.

Craig's books are unusual and original for their insights and unlikely connections.

A more traditional approach to social commentary is taken in *Scotland In The 20th Century* (EUP), a survey of the massive changes this century has brought to Scotland. T M Devine and R J Finlay have collected articles by some of Scotland's leading commentators to provide an overview of trends in the diverse fields of literature, housing, education, land ownership and de-industrialisation. It's a shame too many contributors take a dry, academic tone. The book suffers from having no unifying narrative and comes across ultimately as a somewhat prosaic exercise.

More useful for future sociologists would be *Roots In A Northern Landscape* (Scottish Cultural Press, £7.95), a volume celebrating memories of childhood forty to sixty years ago in North East Scotland, put together by W Gordon Lawrence. A diverse squad of contributors, including Stuart Hood, Raymond Vettese, and David Kerr Cameron, take on a common theme of the growth of consciousness and concurrent loss of innocence in the form of reminiscences, thoughts and observations.

Bonnie Prince Charlie's landing on Eriskay in 1745 drew the world's attention to the Hebrides for the first time. The islands' isolation and way of life were irrevocably shattered. *The Discovery of the Hebrides* by Elizabeth Bray (Birlinn, £12.99) tells of the exploration and exploitation of one of Britain's most beautiful regions during voyages between 1745 and 1883 in excerpts from records and journals of visitors, and the poems and songs of the Hebrideans, detailing a way of life now lost.

Another book on the history of the Scottish Islands is *The Lewis Land Struggle* by Joni Buchanan (Acair), which explains how the Isle of Lewis has retained a substantial rural population because its people resisted landlordism, insisting on the right to remain on the land they occupied. Without these struggles the crofting population would have been eliminated as it was elsewhere. Buchanan writes passionately and convincingly from the crofters' point of view. Unashamedly partisan, she aims to remember and honour the heroes of the struggle.

It was on the Islands the Vikings exerted their greatest influence, and *Scottish Skalds and Sagamen* by Julian D'Arcy (Tuckwell Press, £14.99) examines the influence of Old Norse literature, including the legends of Odin, Thor, Loki and the other gods of Asgard, on Scottish writers down the ages. This is a detailed and exhaustive academic study taking in Lewis Grassic Gibbon, Neil M Gunn, Hugh MacDiarmid, Naomi Mitchison and George Mackay Brown, among others.

Allan H MacLaine examines another thread of Scottish literature in *The Christis Kirk Tradition* (ASLS, £25.00). This is the first anthology of the most important poems of the Christis Kirk genre. Twenty long poems are included, covering the period from the Fifteenth Century to Burns. The essence of the Christis Kirk poems lies in the swift, loose satirical narratives of festivities and ribald revelries. Written in a form that is both traditional and complex, the poems deserve their place in the history of Scots poetry.

Aberdeen City Council have published a facsimile of a 1912 edition of Gavin Greig's popular rural saga *Mains's Wooin'*, a play with music reflecting life in Aberdeenshire a hundred years ago. Greig was a playwright, poet and composer as well as a folk song collector of international repute. This book should have been typeset anew, as the old text is tightly crammed and faintly printed, therefore difficult to read.

Another worthwhile project which disappoints is Leah Leneman's *Into The Foreground* (NMS, £9.99). Her aim is a visual record of the lives of ordinary women in Scotland over the past one hundred years, and her collection of photographs portrays hard work, strength and humour amid the contrasts of class and background, and domestic and community environments. It's a pity these mostly dull, unremarkable photos are unable to carry the weight of the book's ambition.

The one item in this Catalogue I rate essential is not a book at all, but a CD of James Kelman reading *Seven Stories* (AK Audio). It's all relatively early work, nothing less than ten years old, which is a slight disappointment, but Kelman's low-key, unaffected delivery draws the listener in, particularly on the two longer tracks. We are fortunate to have a record of arguably Scotland's greatest living novelist telling his stories like this.

Kelman's concern for authors who are victims of oppression leads us to *Voices Of Conscience* (Iron Press, £12.99), a worldwide collection of poems on the theme of state tyranny by over one hundred and fifty twentieth Century poets. State oppression is also an important theme of Miroslav Holub, the Czech Republic's most important and well-known contemporary poet, and his *Poems Before and After* (Bloodaxe, £9.95) covers thirty years of his poetry.

Of more permanent value is James MacPherson's edition of the *Poems of Ossian* (EUP), undoubtedly one of the most influential literary works to have emerged from the British Isles. It's shocking that no usable modern version has been available until now.

In an odd twist on the historical novel, Clark Geddes has based *Nemesis In The Mearns* (Scottish Cultural Press, £9.99) on real life characters and events in the lifetime of major Scottish novelist, Lewis Grassic Gibbon.

Willa Muir and Catherine Carswell have not gone down as yet among greats like LGG, but Canongate classics are trying to put right that oversight by publishing their neglected works. Willa Muir's *Imagined Selves* (£8.99) gathers together some of the real and imagined lives of one of the finest female intellectuals Scotland has produced this century. Most of her works have been out of print more than fifty years and others have never yet been published. Catherine Carswell's *Lying Awake* (£5.99) is an autobiography left incomplete at her death and edited into shape by her son. The book was never intended to be a simple narrative of her own life, but an attempt to stake out her position in childhood and in old age and stretch the threads of her life in between. It's a strange technique that ignores her most active years of success and influence.

Finally a mention for a colourful set of posters produced by the National Museum of Scotland which address the problem of how to illustrate poetry with some style. Some of these posters can be seen displayed on the walls surrounding the building site of the National Museum. Displace pop stars and footballers from your bedroom wall with some aonghas macneacail, Robert Burns or George Mackay Brown.

John Edwards

Notes on Contributors

Sheena Blackhall has published 18 books to date, 6 of which are short story collections, the remainder being poetry mainly in Doric/North East Scots.

Gavin Bowd is author of a booklet of poems, *Decades*, and an essay, *The Outsiders: Alexander Trocchi and Kenneth White*.

Narcís Comadira considers painting to be his real vocation. Born in 1942, he published his first collection of poems in 1969 and continues to be a crucial presence on the poetic scene while also painting, drawing and writing for the theatre.

John Edwards was born in Birkenhead, has lived in London, Exeter and now in Edinburgh. He is working on a series of publications about Celtic art and culture.

Gabriel Ferrater who died in 1972 at the age of 50, was an outstanding critic and a linguist as well as a major poet. His three collections were brought together in 1979 under the heading of *Les dones i els dies*. The brilliant concision of his essays and lectures on Riba, Foix and Carner have acquired for them the status of modern classics.

Rody Gorman born Dublin 1960. Lives in Skye. His collection *Fax and Other Poems* was published by *Polygon* in 1996.

Paula Jennings writes poetry, published in a number of anthologies and magazines. Is a massage therapist and lives in Edinburgh.

Simon King-Spooner: born London 1948, lives and works in Edinburgh. One story published previously in *Metropolitan*. Latterly exploring ways of failing to write a novel.

C J Lindsay: The Cat is still scaring people (in work and writing!) Recommends The Bookstop Café, Edin. for books and amazing food.

George McKissock: undistinguished occasional writer of short stories, poems and pantomime scripts. Glaswegian now resident in magical islands of Orkney. Lover of sea, hills and standing stones.

Andrew McNeil: born Toledo, Ohio. Bred from an early age in the East Neuk of Fife. Not surprised to find some Cheyenne in his bloodlines. Written poetry in Scots – work due in *Northwords*, trying hard in prose.

Maria-Mercé Marçal, born in 1952, is the leading Catalan women poet of her generation. Her first six collections appeared in one volume as *Llengua abolida* in 1989. In 1994 she published her first, award-winning novel *La passió segons Renée Vivien*.

Josep Maria Murgades teaches Catalan at the Central University in Barcelona and is an expert on the standardisation of the Catalan language at the hands of Pompeu Fabra.

Quim Monzó and **Sergi Pàmies** have gained enormous popularity with novels and shorter fiction describing life in present day Barcelona in all its rich, confusing, postmodernist complexity. The detached, disenchanted tone does not, however, exclude an underlying, serious, satirical intent.

Emma Pitcairn is an unemployed graduate who stays sane by volunteering at Chapman. Open to any job offers.

Neus Real is attached to the Autonomous University in Barcelona. Her research interests are in Catalan's women's writing in general, with a special focus on the earlier part of the 20th century.

Leslie Schenk returned to his writing career mid-1993 after a long hiatus in UN service in various countries around the world, and has already had twenty new acceptances in the UK and the US.

Paul Scott is a former diplomat who has been active in Scottish affairs since his return to Edinburgh. His latest book is *Scotland: An Unwon Cause* (Canongate).

Gerry Stewart is an adopted Scot who is currently on a bus somewhere between Edinburgh and Glasgow, trying to write poetry on the beauty of a bumpy motorway.

Arseny Tarkovsky (1907-1989) became known in the West after his inclusion of his poems in the films of his son Andrei. A friend of Ahkmatova and Tsvetayeva, he was the most respected of the older generation of poets who lived to see the era of 'glasnost'.

Lluís-Maria Todó's third novel, *L'Adoració perpètua*, has just been published. He is an expert on French literature and teaches translation studies at the Pompeu Fabra University.

Christopher Whyte has just published his second novel, *The Warlock of Strathearn*, with Gollancz and his third, *The Gay Decameron*, is due out next spring.

Jim C Wilson: second poetry collection – *Cellos in Hell* (*Chapman*). Runs poetry workshops for Edinburgh University. Hates crowds, so gives poetry readings.